MURDER ON THE MESA

A Violet Vaughn Southwestern Mystery #1

Kristina Charles

ULM Publishing

ISBN: 9798398461169

Cover design by: ULM Publishing
Library of Congress Control Number: 2018675309
Printed in the United States of America

CONTENTS

CHAPTER 1

The rickety RV chugged up the steep mountain slope as if it were pulling ten loaded freight cars. The ticking noise that popped up a few miles back wasn't a good sign. Tick-tick. Tick-tick. Tick-tick. Violet leaned forward, as if the extra pull would force the churning machine upward. Tick-tick. Tick-tick. Through gritted teeth, she spoke in rhythm to the Tick-tick sound. "Gonna. Kill him. Gonna. Kill him. Gonna. Kill him." Alone in the beat up rig, her heart became the baseline to her Tick-tick song. It was playing sixteenth notes.

Violet's first time behind the wheel of an RV came seven hours ago as she headed out of Chicago. When she bought the thing off Craigslist yesterday, she mainly focused on cleaning it out. Apparently its last incarnation was a party wagon carrying twenty-something college kids from DePaul University to Burning Man. It survived that excursion, just barely. But at $2,000, it was the cheapest thing she could find that actually ran. The young man who sold it to her seemed nice enough.

He looked at her skeptically when she arrived as he took in her appearance. She imagined that absolutely nothing about her said "RV". Not her groomed black bob with precision straight bangs, red lipstick, cream blazer and patent stilettos. Nor her age—she could be his mother, and then some. And then there was her lack of an accompanying man, although most of the college kids nowadays are too PC to point any of those things out. Yes, she knew he was wondering why this attractive, put-together, middle-aged woman wanted to drive a dumpy old frat-wagon that smelled like beer and dirty socks.

"Don't you want to look under the hood, ma'am? Or see the holding tank?" The poor kid seemed reluctant to let her just take him at his word that the RV was in working order, so she let him show her all the pertinent features. But her eyes glazed over while he was talking about black waste and gray waste, electrical hookups and storage space. She was so pissed at Jim and what he had done that it was hard to focus on these details.

"You know ma'am, if you want to spend just a little more money, you can get something a lot nicer than this. I mean, it runs alright and will get you there, but…" He trailed off as they toured the inside of the vehicle. Violet thought he was sweet. If she had had children, she would have liked to have a son like this. She could tell he cared about people, and that was a quality she cherished. She'd had an abundance of the opposite kind of person in her life, so when she encountered kindness, she accepted it with gratitude.

"You're a nice young man," she said sincerely. "Thanks for your concern, but I know what I'm doing." This was certainly a lie, in the RV department anyway, but she had to get going. The kid had no way of knowing she would have to practically drain her account to buy the vehicle. She might look well off, but in reality she was just shy of poor with a rich woman's wardrobe. The second hand clothes business had that perk anyway.

After the RV, there would be a little left over for supplies and gas, but not much. She'd have to be savvy with every cent, but she'd been doing that for the past ten years and was a pro by now. Her next paycheck would land in her account in a week. Hopefully by that time she could do what she needed to do.

She paid the kid in cash and gave him an extra twenty to drive the RV over to her place. She worked late into the night, cleaning, scrubbing and outfitting the old beast with everything she could grab from her apartment. Her white tornado revealed 1 the Winnebago had surprisingly good bones. The addition of some plush bedding and bright pillows gave the inside a respectable, albeit dated, appearance.

Now, as the RV churned up the mountain, Violet thought back to when the kid was showing her the engine. What did he say? "A little slow on the grades, don't force it, it'll get you there. Runs like a dream on the flats." He was right. It had been smooth sailing heading down through Illinois, which gave her some time to get used to driving the high profile vehicle.

She found that driving on the highway wasn't too bad. It was city traffic and parking that stressed her out. For the couple of pit stops en route, she located a Walmart and found places in the distant areas of the parking lot where she could pull in across spaces and not have to back up.

The slopes got steep and steeper just as she left St. Louis. The Winnebago groaned in protest, a whale swimming upstream. The tick-tick seemed to be growing louder. Her high heeled boot shook on the accelerator, adrenaline coursing through her. It was on this slope that the total mistake of this journey set in. But what else could she do? Jim totally screwed her over. She had never really travelled, barely even leaving the Chicago area in her 50 years. The aching struggle up the slope felt like a metaphor for her life. And a lot of that came down to Jim too. I'm a completely different person now, she tried to tell herself. I'm not trapped anymore. But the specter of Jim planted itself right back in her mind, scaring her all over again.

She saw a sign up ahead. Gray Summit. Shaw Nature Reserve. RV Park. Next Right. Did that say summit? "Halleluja!" She cried. "We're gonna make it!" By now, she and the worn Winnebago were a team and she was beginning to have real affection for the thing. She turned off at the exit and found herself surrounded by green, grassy meadows. She located the sign for the RV park and followed a gravel road that wound through a dense forest, the trees coloring beautifully in the early fall.

The gravel road ended at a little wooden house with a sign that said "office". Violet jumped out and stretched for a moment. Her legs were still a little weak and tingly from her panicky climb up the mountain. As she walked toward the office, her high-heeled boots sunk into the gravel and she almost twisted her ankle on the short walk. These were the most rugged footwear she owned. With her jeans tucked into the tall boots and an LL Bean sweater, this was the closest she came to roughing it.

A small, dusty man with gray hair and a long gray beard came out the office door and seemed to freeze in place as he took in Violet and the RV.

"You lookin to stay?" he said, with a great deal of uncertainty.

"Yes," she said, drawing her shoulders back and affecting the confident, professional demeanor she worked hard to perfect. "How much is it?" The man was peering over her shoulder, at the RV.

"You and your husband?" RV park owners in Missouri were obviously not as PC as Chicago college students.

"No." Noticing for the first time the complete lack of any other soul in view, she quickly revised her answer. "Um, yes. He's resting in the back. He's—"

"Oh, you two's not married, eh?" The man chuckled. "We ain't that old fashioned around here." He gave her a wink. "Come on in the office."

After taking her payment, he handed her a print out map of the park with little numbered squares. He circled the number 12 in red pen. She looked it over, trying to get her bearings.

"So...that's it?" She asked.

"Yup. Tell your boyfriend that number 12 is a tight fit, but I need to keep the bigger spots open, they'll be folks showin up later this evening, most likely." She didn't like the sound of that, but she took her map and headed back to her rig. Tight fit? How hard could it be?

Forty five minutes later, as she inched the RV backwards yet again, aiming for the concrete slab that now appeared to be the size of a saltine, she understood tight fit. Her initial thoughts of just driving forward onto the slab were dashed when she realized the hookups were on the opposite side. It was getting dark and she had already clipped a garbage can and barely missed a picnic table. Some campers across the way—apparently hunters judging by their camo getup—had a front row seat to her misery. They downed beers in their folding chairs, their bushy beards bouncing with laughter as they enjoyed the spectacle.

"Jerks," she whispered under her breath. She finally turned off the engine and got out to check her position. It was a little too close to the hookup box for comfort, but it would have to do. She was starving and she still needed to hook the RV up to all the—stuff. And it was getting dark. Using her phone flashlight, she peered inside the cupboard the kid had droned on about. She realized her aloneness in that moment. It can't be worse than walking through West Garfield Park, she thought, and she had done that at night a few times. But being totally out of her element had her senses on high alert.

The stretchy tubing for the plumbing was a confusing lump and she couldn't remember where the electric cable was. She fumbled and swore and kept dropping the phone.

"Need some help?" Violet jumped sky high. Her boot heel lodged in the gravel and she stumbled back, nearly falling into the open side panel. She registered a man in a blue sweater vest. Killers usually didn't wear sweater vests, she thought. And was that a British accent?

"Sorry about that, didn't mean to frighten you. It just looked like you might be a newbie to RVing."

"Oh, um, well. I should be okay," she lied. She didn't want a strange man to know she was clueless out here, sweater vest or not.

He smiled a bit, but kindly. "First rule of RVing. Never turn down help. I was you about a month ago and I never would have made it without help from strangers."

Her shoulders slumped and she sat down on the edge of the open cabinet. The man's kind face and offer of help brought tears to her eyes. After the emotional rollercoaster of the past few days, tears threatened to spring out and she knew if she started, it was going to be an ugly cry.

"Yes," she whispered. "I need help. If you're a serial killer, just let me have a cocktail and a meal before you kill me, I don't want to die hungry and in need of a drink."

He smiled broadly and extended a hand. "I'm Hugh."

"Violet." She took his hand and he helped her up.

"I'm not a serial killer, more like a serial helper. How about this," he said as he began straightening out the tubing. "I'll get you hooked up quickly right now, and in the morning I can talk you through it, when we have more light. It's not as confusing as it looks, after you've done it a couple of times."

He didn't say *why the hell are you out here by yourself with no clue what you're doing?* And he had a sense of humor. That made him okay in her book. "Sounds perfect," she said, and she followed him around giving him some light with her phone.

In short order, they were inside the RV, with Hugh checking light switches and turning on the tap. "I think you're all set for now," he said, giving the place a final look around. "You got the retro look going on in here, I like it." There was a slight twinkle in his eye, but she couldn't blame him for teasing her. At least it no longer smelled like beer and armpits.

They stood outside once more and Violet shook Hugh's hand gratefully. "I was going to invite you to sit outside for some wine and cheese in thanks, but I just realized I don't have any chairs. Or—any other, what do you call it, outside stuff."

He raised an eyebrow. "Do you have wine and cheese?"

"Of course. I only brought essentials."

"Well I'm set up over in space ten and I have

outside stuff, as you call it. I even have a little fire pit I could set up. Why don't you bring your wine and cheese over and you can tell me how you found yourself here."

Violet's guard went up. What could she possibly tell him about her situation and where she was going? But she was also tired. Of everything. She hadn't just sat and had a drink with someone in a long time, and something about Hugh felt, well, friendly. Everyone probably felt that way around him. He was just—nice.

"Okay, let me get cleaned up, I'll be over in a few." As soon as she was back in the RV, she immediately flopped onto the queen bed. "I need better shoes!" she said out loud, but all she had were high heels and her fluffy pink slippers. She allowed her body to relax for a minute and thought about Hugh the good Samaritan. I wonder what his story is, she thought. There's probably a Mrs. Hugh back at his campsite. He appeared to be about her age, tall with graying blond hair, clean shaven and a neat and crisp appearance. And what was with the accent?

A vision came into her mind, a hand coming up to slap her. Cowering. Being mocked for cowering. She shook her head. This business with Jim was bringing it all up to the surface, what she had worked so hard to push down. What had her counselor told her? H.A.L.T., that was it. Hungry, angry, lonely, tired. That's when we're most vulnerable. I can put a check mark on each one of those, she thought.

A short time later she padded across the dirt

in her pink slippers, carrying the wine, a round of brie and some crackers. At the number ten camp site, she was met with a picture right off the cover of Outdoorsman magazine. Hugh's modern RV sparkled. A cheerful awning, sparkling with little white lights, stretched out over a rug, table and chairs. The promised fire pit crackled merrily. Hugh stood next to the fire pit, and waved her over.

"I see you've got your hiking shoes on," he said, glancing at the fluffy pink shoewear.

"Let's just say I'm not really outdoorsy," she said, coming to stand next to the fire.

"And yet, here you are. Maybe you're more outdoorsy than you think." He busied himself moving the chairs and table closer to the fire pit while Violet uncorked the wine and poured it into paper cups and sliced up some cheese. They both sat and Violet raised her glass to him. "To new friends."

"To mysterious strangers," he said, raising his. "I find myself in a place of dying to know what your story is. But being rude and intrusive goes against everything it is to be English. So maybe you can help me out and not make me ask."

"No, you first, Mr. British accent in—where are we again?"

"Shaw Nature Reserve. Missouri. United States."

"Okay, if you say so. Are you a travel writer or something?"

"No, I'm a therapist."

To Violet, that made sense, and yet made no

sense at all. "So you really are a serial helper."

"Yes, I really am. Pathologically so. But that doesn't really explain what I'm doing here, does it? Let's just say I came to America five weeks ago to get my daughter settled into college at NYU. And then…I didn't want to go back home."

Violet noted the sadness that passed across his face. "So you bought an RV and started travelling around a strange country by yourself?"

"Actually, travelling around in an RV had been the plan my wife and I had for years." Hugh threw little pieces of leaves into the fire and they both watched as they smoked and sparkled.

"Did she change her mind or did something happen to her?" Violet asked quietly.

Hugh chuckled, but it sounded harsh and a little mocking. "Something happened to her alright, yeah, you could say that. For the past few years she seemed so distant. I mean, she was always kind of cold and distant, but she was more distant than usual. She said she was having a hard time with menopause. So, stupid me, I joined a Facebook group of menopausal women so I could figure out how to help her."

"Why stupid? That sounds like a nice thing to do."

"Stupid, because while I was getting advice on Facebook and reading menopause books, she was boffing my best friend. Sorry, that may not be a word over here."

"I get the gist," said Violet. "I'm sorry." They sat in silence for awhile. Then Violet said, "So what kind of therapist are you?"

Hugh straightened up and looked her in the eye. "Marriage." All at once, they both burst out laughing and the seriousness was broken. Violet poured more wine and finally said, "It's funny, but my story has to do with a marriage too." As the image of Jim came into her mind, a chill passed through her and any lightness she felt disappeared.

Hugh noticed the look on her face. "You okay?"

"Yes. I guess this is the danger of talking to a therapist, it's hard to hide my feelings."

"Hiding feelings is what leads to a great deal of human misery," he said, sounding very therapisty. "That's why I shared my story with you, and I've shared it with others. Speaking it aloud takes away its weight. I think you have a story to tell, one that is weighing you down. Why don't you talk to me about it? We're just two strangers meeting in the night."

Violet smiled and felt her shoulders drop. "My story is a little convoluted."

Hugh smiled at her. "It's 8 p.m., we have a nice fire and wine. "I'm ready for a good story."

CHAPTER 2

Violet often wondered how her mother had the wherewithal to give her such a colorful name. Actually, she couldn't picture her mother naming a baby at all. The image of a woman lovingly cradling a newborn didn't compute with the angry, absent and often out of it single mother she'd grown up with. She gave Hugh an overview of those dark times and then sat in silence for a while.

"I thought Jim was the answer," she said finally, staring into the fire.

"It didn't work out that way?"

"Hardly. I jumped out of the frying pan and—well, you know."

Hugh nodded, sadly. "Unfortunately, I do. Hazard of the job. He was abusive?"

Her heart rate began to rise as images bubbled up out of the recesses she had them stored. A sardonic face, forced up close to hers and hot breath breathing words, *you're nothing, nothing*.

She remembered the man in front of her, gazing at her, not with sympathy, but with sorrow, or maybe even relatability, in his eyes. "Abusive. Yes. Psychologically, emotionally abusive. The worst thing was he made me think I was crazy. Twenty years of head games. And controlling to the point I was a prisoner in my own home. But what a home it was," she said wistfully. "We bought it as a fixer-upper when Jim was just out of law school. Then I spent a good portion of my life restoring it. By the time I left, the neighborhood had become desirable and the house was worth a fortune. But I left it—and everything I owned—to live in a shelter."

Hugh leaned forward, surprised. "A homeless shelter?"

"A domestic violence shelter."

"Wow. That took some courage."

"I was really beaten down, I didn't feel courageous. But looking back—yeah, it took all the courage I had."

"How long did you stay at the shelter?"

"In some ways, I never left. When I first got to the shelter—actually, it's called The Healing Place —I needed stuff to wear and they showed me a storage room where they kept all the donations. The room was crammed full of garbage bags. To keep myself busy, I started sorting through the clothes and hanging them up, organizing them. The management bought some racks, and next thing you know, I had a little store. Lots of wealthy women donated clothes so we had some nice stuff. The store generated money right off the bat and pretty soon we expanded. As of now, we have four stores in Chicago, all profitable.

And I manage them all."

"That's an amazing story. Riches to rags to riches." The admiration in his eyes was real.

"More like riches to rags to getting by."

"It still doesn't explain what you're doing out here," Hugh said with some humor.

"I know, I'm getting off track, but it will all make sense. So right from the start, Jim said he wouldn't give me a divorce and I didn't have the money to fight him. I never had any money of my own, he controlled everything. But my name was on the house title. I carried that thought with me in my heart for ten years. It was my nest egg, my security."

"So you're still married?" Hugh prodded.

"I never think of it as being married since we haven't spoken in a decade. But technically, yes. Over the years, I would drive by the house when I knew Jim wouldn't be there. Just to see it, to know I had something in this world with my name on it. Then, last week, I found out that Jim screwed me over."

Hugh's eyes went wide. "What happened?"

I drove by and there were people out in the yard, and kids. It was surreal. I wondered what they were doing there. Turns out, Jim sold the house! He must have forged my signature."

"It also would have to be witnessed by at least a notary," said Hugh.

"Yes, that's something else to look into. But there's bigger problems. I went to his office to confront him, and get this—the FBI was there. He's being investigated for fraud! He was stealing his clients' settlements. He's a personal injury lawyer, so these are sad cases, like people maimed and paralyzed. Special Agent Montoya from the FBI seemed completely disgusted by Jim and I think she sees me as guilty by association."

"But you haven't been with him for years."

"Exactly. I told her he sold the house out from under me and stole my money. She just told me to get in line, he stole a lot of people's money. But the thing is, he's missing. And I'm the only one who knows where he is."

"And I take it you're not going to share that information with Special Agent Montoya."

"Right. Well not yet. I need to try to get my money. Then I'll turn him in."

"So where are you going? Don't worry, I won't say anything. I'm a foreigner, it's none of my business. But I do hope that bloody moron gets what's coming to him."

Violet was hesitant. It had been good to get this story off her chest, but she didn't know how much she could trust Hugh. On the other hand, she hadn't told anyone else, so if she disappeared off the face of the planet, no one would ever know where she ended up. Finally she uttered one word.

"Coatimundi."

Hugh looked puzzled. "I'm sorry, what?"

"The place. Coatimundi. It's a weird name, but I've remembered it all these years." She sounded it out. "Co-ah-tee-moon-dee. Jim told me the word is some kind of animal they have in New Mexico. He tried to describe it, but I honestly don't know what it is, he said it's some kind of cross between a raccoon and a bear and a monkey."

"And he wasn't pulling your leg?"

"Maybe. But not about the town. A long time ago he told me about this place he found when he was just out of college. It's in the middle of nowhere and there's a mesa where all sorts of weird people live, folks that live off the grid. He was so taken with the town he bought a little piece of land. He said there's nothing on his plot but an old rusted out windmill. He said it's a place where someone could disappear. I know that's where he's gone."

"And you're going after him?" Hugh sounded doubtful.

"I've been standing in line all my life. And for once, I have leverage," she said.

"If he doesn't give you your money, you turn him in?"

"That's the plan. But I'll turn him in eventually."

"It sounds very—dangerous," said Hugh.

"My life with my mother and with Jim were dangerous. And—I've been foolish. I should have settled things long ago. But I was afraid. I'm trying to reinvent myself. I'm tired of being a shrinking violet."

Hugh laughed at the pun, but then said seriously, "You've made a new life. Why put yourself at risk? Walk away."

Violet stood up from her chair and stretched. The RV travel had sunk into her bones and she was achy and tired.

"You're a nice guy, Hugh. Your wife didn't deserve you. Thanks for listening to my story. I'm gonna turn in, I have to leave early."

Hugh stood up as well. "Sorry if I was too direct, I have that problem sometimes. Come and get me in the morning and I'll show you the ropes with the hookups."

"Okay, I'd appreciate it. Goodnight Hugh."

In the morning, Hugh, looking clean and pressed in a yellow sweater vest and khakis, showed her the hook ups step by step while Violet shot a video with her phone. She noticed that his camping spot was all cleared out, his rig ready to hit the road.

"Where ya headed?" she asked.

"You know, I'm getting a little bored and lonely roaming around aimlessly by myself. I've heard about this animal in New Mexico that's a cross between a raccoon, a bear and a monkey. I thought I might see if I can find one. Could you do with a wingman?"

CHAPTER 3

It wasn't easy finding Coatimundi. The little wagon train of two RVs stopped at numerous four way junctions where they checked both GPS and paper maps. Eventually they crested a hill and saw the mesa laid out before them. Hugh's RV was in the lead of course. Violet's vehicle, Winnie as she had dubbed her, came huffing and puffing up behind. The mesa below spread out for miles. In the early evening Violet was struck by the reds, purples and pinks of the sage-strewn sand, craggy rock formations and hills. Homes and ranches dotted the mesa and the road appeared to be heading for a small town situated at the edge of the desert.

A large art installation on the outskirts of town appeared to be made of hundreds of mis-matched dining chairs, all stacked and painted random colors. On the main street—or maybe the only street—a gun shop with pictures of machine guns and American flags was sandwiched between a bead shop in full-on hippie tie dye colors and a Coffee shop called "Coati Coffee".

Violet followed Hugh to the RV park they

located online. They drove past a hand-painted wooden sign that read Maven's Haven and into the parking lot of a vintage, L-shaped motel where an enormous metal Lizard posed out front. Toward the back, Violet could see an open area for RVs.

In the office they were met by Maven herself, a tall woman, her silver hair in two braids, dressed in denim and dripping in turquoise jewelry.

"So y'all are needing two spaces then?" Maven said, pulling out some paperwork. "Where you from? You here for Mundi Madness?"

Both Violet and Hugh were struck dumb for a moment. Violet assumed Hugh, like herself, was wishing they had invented a cover story.

"Nottingham, England," Hugh said finally. "Yes, here for the um—madness."

"England, is that right?" Maven said, pausing from her paperwork. "It's gonna be the best one ever this year. I should know, I'm head of the committee. But I didn't realize our fame had reached all the way to England. And you, hon, you from England too?"

"Chicago."

"Chicago! Well now, that's a kick. We have some other folks that just came in from Chicago too." Violet and Hugh exchanged glances.

"Oh, really?" Said Violet. "They're here for the Mundi Madness too?"

"No, I don't think so. A pushy bunch, came in asking a lot of questions, do I know this person, tryin to show me pictures of somebody, who knows. I said folks around here don't take kindly to a lot of questions. One of the guys looks like a cop, so you can bet I shut my trap right up. Here you go, spaces 15 and 16. Wifi password is big lizard."

Violet thought quickly about how to get some information without making Maven suspicious.

"I do have a couple of questions, but not nosey ones." Violet gave Maven her best smile. "I'm an artist. I paint windmills. Of all shapes and sizes, preferably old ones. You have anything like that around here?"

"I'm an artist myself, sculptures, like the lizard out there," Maven pointed. That's what Mundi Madness is all about, right? Let me think now, windmills you say?"

"Out by Three Peaks," came a voice from the back office.

"My wife Maddie," said Maven, nodding toward the door. "She knows everything about the mesa people." A woman with short pink hair poked her head around the corner.

"There's a beat up old windmill out by Three Peaks. That's West side of the mesa. You head that direction and you'll see three pointy hills. There's a few homesteads out there, but it's tricky to get to. I can draw you a map if it would help."

"Absolutely," said Violet, "that would be perfect. Also, is there anywhere around here we could rent a car?"

Maven laughed. "Like Avis or something? No, nothing like that. But tell you what. For an extra ten dollars a day, you can drive that old beater in the parking lot." Violet and Hugh looked out the window and saw the beater was an old Ford pickup that might have once been green, but was now a mottled mix of olive green and rust.

"We'll take it," said Violet. "And Maven, one more thing. We'd also like to, you know—steer clear of the cop."

Maven gave them a knowing wink. "What happens in Coatimundi, stays in Coatimundi. They're in rooms seven and eight in the motel."

Hugh and Violet set up their camps quickly, and met under Hugh's canopy for cheese and wine, as was becoming their habit. "Nottingham? Seriously? As in Robin Hood? That's too perfect," teased Violet.

"I'm afraid I left my bow and arrow back home, but I could don some tights if you'd like," Hugh said while scrolling through his phone. "Here it is. Mundi Madness is a celebration of Southwest art and culture," he read from his phone. "Three days of food, entertainment and art displays culminating in the Midnight Moon Dance."

"It gives us an excuse to be here," said Violet. "But my art skills are limited to stick figures. I hope I'm not called upon to produce anything."

Hugh jumped up from his chair. "Hang on." He returned in a moment with a case that, when opened, contained a fold-up easel and paints. "I had a grand ambition I would travel America and learn to paint," he said. "But this has never been out of the box, so you can see how that's going."

"Good thinking," said Violet, I'll set it up outside

Winnie. "Seriously though, I have to focus on what I'm here for. I need to find Jim, confront him and get my money before I lose the nerve."

"Apparently you're not the only person who knows about Jim's hideout. It sounded like that group from Chicago might be here for the same reason you are."

"I don't know how that's possible," said Violet. "Maybe it's just a coincidence."

"We can't set out for that Three Peaks place until morning, it's almost dark," said Hugh. "I say we see what we can find out about the Chicago people tonight and then look for the windmill in the morning."

"You say 'we'. This is my battle to fight with Jim. I don't want you having to get involved in all the messiness. I can go by myself tomorrow."

"Not bloody likely," said Hugh. "What kind of wingman leaves the ace pilot hanging at the critical hour? No, I'm in this with you now, no going back."

Hugh did some more scrolling on his phone and Violet took a moment to surreptitiously glance at him. He was the most comfortable person to be with that she had ever met. He got her. That was hard to find. She was also starting to notice that he was kind of handsome. The sleeves of his oxford shirt were rolled up to show strong forearms and—stop it, Violet, she thought. Nope. You need a friend a lot more than you need a boyfriend. Then she realized Hugh was talking to her.

"Look, over there. Rooms 7 and 8 are heading out." Past the expanse of the sagebrush-covered RV park, one branch of the motel was visible, and sure enough, both room doors stood open and a small group of people could be seen putting on jackets and talking together. They closed their room doors and starting walking toward the road.

"Let's go," said Hugh. The night was growing chilly, so they quickly grabbed their own jackets, locked their RVs and headed after the group. They walked down the main street, passing businesses both quirky (Frog's Eye Herbs and Vices) and practical (Sunset Title). They saw the group enter a restaurant, Badlands Barbecue.

"Perfect," said Hugh.

"Why perfect, you think it's a good place to spy?"

"That and I'm sick of cheese and crackers. I need some real food."

As the barbecue smell hit her, Violet began to salivate, overwhelmed by the same feeling. When was the last time she had a real meal? Inside, a band played underneath a banner that said "The Madness Begins." They grabbed a booth right behind the Chicago group. Two of the party, both men, sat at the booth, while the woman circulated, showing a flyer to other patrons. The fourth person, a man, stood at the bar, ordering drinks. A waitress took Hugh and Violet's order, each of them getting the barbecue rib special.

Violet slid to the edge of the booth. "Okay, I'm gonna head up to the bar and try to chat that guy up. You wait here and see if the woman approaches our table with the flyer."

Violet sat on a barstool next to the man, who was looking at his phone. He appeared to be in his thirties, so Violet wasn't sure if a flirty approach would work, but maybe the guy liked cougars. "Was that a Chicago accent I heard earlier?" she said in what she hoped was a sultry voice. The guy stopped checking out his phone and looked her over.

"I can tell by how you say Chicago you would know," he said in a friendly way. "You from Chi-town?"

His brain looked like it was slowly computing stuff, so Violet quickly said, "Yeah, I'm here for the Mundi Madness."

"Oh yeah? That's cool," he said. Violet hadn't been prepared for him to be friendly and open. She had been thinking of these people as scary, but she realized all she had were assumptions about them, with no evidence, other than Maven saying they were pushy. "You here for the festival as well?" she asked.

"Me? No, I never even heard of it, or Cotty Moody, or whatever you call it, until recently. I'm here with my sister and my brother. We're trying to find a guy."

This is going great, Violet thought, what do I say to not blow it? "Ohhh, that sounds mysterious," she said. "Are you a detective?" Ugh, that sounds stupid, she thought, but it didn't seem to phase him.

"No, C.J. over there is the detective." He pointed toward the table, at a guy who she was certain Maven had picked out as the cop.

"He's helping us find the guy who stole my

25

mom's money. She was in an accident. She's messed up," he said, starting to get emotional. Violet noticed he had two empty shot glasses sitting in front of him.

"Oh really, how terrible," she said sympathetically. This was obviously one of the poor families that Jim had defrauded. She felt strangely guilty, like she was somehow responsible for Jim. "Who is this guy? What's he doing in this place?"

"Some ambulance chaser," he said, now sounding angry. "Thought he would sneak out of town with my mom's money now that the feds are on him. Well my sister works in IT and is an expert in cell phone data. She tracked him better than the feds could. But she can only track it to this area, so now we're trying to find him." Just then the sister walked up, with an unpleasant look on her face. This must be the pushy one, Violet thought.

"Are you drinking again Junior? I thought you were gonna cool it." She grabbed his arm. Violet said a quick "good luck" and headed back to the table where the ribs had just been set down. She and Hugh shared a look and a nod, which was all that was needed to convey, "Yup, they're looking for Jim."

CHAPTER 4

Around nine the next morning, Violet and Hugh bounced down a rocky and rutted dirt road in the beat up old pickup. Light had never really come that morning. Storm clouds loomed in a slate gray sky and a piercing wind flattened the sage brush and sent the occasional tumbleweed across their path. Hugh navigated from the passenger seat reading Maddie's hand-drawn map as Violet drove.

"It says we should turn left at the third cattle guard," Hugh said, studying the map. "It seems like ages since the second one."

"On this road, ten feet feels like a mile." Violet gripped the steering wheel so hard, her knuckles were white. Most of her anxiety was not from the driving or the road, but from the prospect of confronting Jim. She was grateful once again to have Hugh with her and she glanced over at him. He was so unlike Jim. Kind, calm, capable. Why was he wasting his time out here with her?

"You know, it's not really about the money," she said, more to shore herself up than anything else. "It's about finally standing up to him."

"Are you expecting him to be out here sitting on top a pile of cash?"

"Actually—yes." Violet realized that's exactly what she thought. "That would be like him. He doesn't trust anybody and needs to have control. I just want what I'm owed, nothing more. But if I can have my say, then it will have meant something to come out here."

"You need to slay the dragon. Metaphorically, that is," Hugh chuckled.

Just then, they saw a cattle guard up ahead and Violet rolled to a stop at the intersection of two dirt roads. "Look!" Violet called, gesturing to left, "At the base of the hills. A windmill."

The windmill was bigger than she had imagined, jutting up out of rocks and sagebrush, dark and rusty.

"Eerie looking old thing, isn't it?" said Hugh. Violet thought she caught some anxiety in his voice too. He was probably regretting this crazy mission. Things had just turned real.

They could see a trailer nearby, a large silver Airstream parked close to the windmill. They drove up the narrow dirt road, a few jack rabbits scattering in front of them. There was an open dirt area out in front of the trailer and not much else. Violet pulled to a stop and they were both quiet as they took in the scene.

"I was thinking." Violet stared at the trailer. "You've already done so much for me, but I was wondering—would you mind saying that you're my lawyer?"

"That sounds like a good idea," Hugh said, zipping up his jacket. "Because I don't think it will have the same feel to say I'm your therapist."

Violet gave a nervous laugh. Hugh put his hand over hers where she was still gripping the steering wheel. "I fancy playing the part of the British barrister, here to defend the rights of my client. I swore to be your wingman to the end. So let's do this."

They got out of the truck and were immediately hit by the chilly wind that raced through the mesa. The old windmill put out a high-pitched squeal. It seemed the rusty thing continued to do its job, despite its age and lack of care. The wind shifted and it emitted a creaky wail as it was forced to change direction.

The Airstream looked brand new. It had the vintage shape of old Airstreams, but this was obviously right off the lot. The stormy sky reflected back at them, captured in the mirror-like shine of the gleaming metal. Strangely, the front door was unlatched and banging in the wind.

"I feel as if we're in an old western and just walked into a ghost town," Hugh whispered.

"For real," Violet whispered back, "this is creepy." Leave it to Jim to want to live in a place like this, she thought.

Violet grabbed the door handle and stopped it from banging, but didn't pull it all the way open. Instead, she rapped on the door and called, "Hello?

Jim?" Nothing.

While they waited, Violet spied a make-shift clothes line out behind the trailer. A woman's red bra and several pairs of panties rippled in the breeze. Whoa, she thought. He's got a woman out here? She knocked again. She could hear rustling coming from inside.

"Can you hear that?" she said. Hugh moved closer to the door. More rustling.

"Yes. Someone's in there."

Violet knocked again and yelled, "I know you're in there. I just want to talk." The rustling stopped. Violet pulled the unlatched door open and was met with semi-darkness. Closed curtains blocked out any light from the overcast morning. Just then, they heard a scratching, rustling sound and Violet could make out a shape moving quickly towards her. No—two shapes—three. She screamed as her legs were jostled by something heavy and she fell back hard against Hugh. Squeals and growls added to the mix as the shapes pushed past them. Violet and Hugh swung around to see three strange animals running away. Larger than a raccoon, the furry beasts appeared more like a small bear or badger, with enormous, fat, striped tails that went straight up in the air.

The bandits scampered away, one dragging a bag of chips with it.

"They must be—"

"Coatimundi," finished Hugh.

"But—what are they—why are they in here?" she said, her voice full of confusion.

Something was very wrong. As soon as they arrived on the property, Violet had sensed things were off. Jim was a loud and boisterous person. He took up space wherever he was, with his voice and his manner. It was too quiet here for Jim. The Jim she knew would have come out to meet the truck, would have been red faced and yelling for her to get off his property.

Violet stepped up and in to the trailer. Hugh followed and switched on his phone flashlight. Violet sucked in her breath. The place was ransacked. They stood in the kitchen area and could see cupboards open, food covering the counters and floor. To their right, cabinets in the living area gaped, clothes and other items spilling out and strewn everywhere.

"I'm no expert, but I don't think coatimundi did all this." Hugh shined the flashlight over the room. "It looks like it's been robbed."

On the edge of the kitchen counter Violet spied a stack of papers. A thick packet on top caught her eye. *For the property at 1070 Fern Ave, Chicago, IL.* The closing papers for her house! This will give me a good opener when I finally find Jim, she thought, shoving the packet into her large purse.

"I'm guessing Jim's not here," Hugh said as he inspected the living room. "He must have got wind of the authorities on his tail and took off."

"You're probably right." Her shoulders slumped. "All of this build up for nothing. But still, what happened here? Someone was looking for something."

"Maybe the Chicago people found out where Jim

was before us and they're looking for the money. Who knows?" said Hugh, "But this place is giving me the willies, let's get out of here."

"Okay, but I want to see what's in the back." She headed down the little hallway toward the bedroom. The wind began to pick up outside. It howled and the trailer shook. The windmill squeaked and clanged, filling the silence as Violet crept toward the half-closed bedroom door. She gently pushed it open and peered in.

Her eyes adjusted to the darkness and she saw the shadowy shape of boxes, stacked in looming towers. A smell triggered her memory. Jim's aftershave. She fought off the urge to retch. Another smell mingled with the cologne, something unpleasant. She turned on her flashlight. More ransacked cabinets and drawers. Her light found the foot of the bed and—wait—cowboy boots. They lay at a strange angle on the bed. Her heart pounded. She slowly moved the flashlight to reveal a man's form. And then she screamed. A knife stuck straight up out of the man's chest.

She had found Jim.

CHAPTER 5

The county sheriff rapped on the window of the truck where earlier a deputy told Violet and Hugh to wait. Rain was just beginning to splatter the windshield.

"Come on out," he said. "Let's go, Mrs. Vaughn." They exited the car and stood in front of the sheriff. He was not at all what Violet expected. People in the sheriff's office in Chicago drove sleek sedans and dressed in crisp tan uniforms, similar to police officers. This sheriff wore jeans and a tie-dye T-shirt that said "Mundi Madness," as well as cowboy boots. He was middle-aged and slim with a hint of five o'clock shadow on his ruggedly handsome face. Still, the face held a hardness that said he wasn't playing.

"That's right, isn't it? Mrs. Violet Vaughn? Wife of the deceased? And her—friend." He looked them both up and down and what he saw did not soften the hardness—or his sarcasm. "I'm Sheriff Winters. Deputy Jones filled me in on your, uh—story."

Violet heard a hint of a Texas drawl and thought he must not be a New Mexico native. "Well I hope he told you that I'm his *estranged* wife. Very estranged," Violet said feeling defensive under his glare.

"Well something is very estranged about this situation," said the sheriff slowly. "Or maybe not so strange. Wife comes in from Chicago with her um—friend," he said with a smirk. "Says she came here to, what was it, have a talk with her *estranged* husband? That's right, instead of picking up the phone, or you know, texting, like we do in the modern world, she gets in an RV and drives halfway across the country to have a conversation. And now he's got a knife in his chest. It might not be so strange after all."

Violet felt a pang in her gut. She had to admit, it did look bad. "He was dead when we got here!" she cried, "And the place was full of those creatures, those —things."

"So you're saying the coati did this?" he shot a look to one of the deputies who shook his head with barely contained laughter. "They are filthy little scavengers, but I never known one to wield a knife."

"Look here," said Violet. "That man in there is at the center of a federal investigation. There's a long list of people who might want him dead, some of them even staying at Maven's place. We've tried to be as helpful as we can, now we just want to go back to town. We're cold and hungry."

The sheriff put his hands on his hips and stared at Violet and Hugh. Deputy Jones looked at them sympathetically, as if he knew what was coming.

"In two days, this valley is gonna be flooded with thousands of people here for Mundi Madness.

And this year, I'm head of the float committee—the meeting from which I just got called out of to deal with you people. I don't like city folks. I don't like Chicago. They have that weird pizza, what do they call it? Deep dish pizza? I like my pizza flat and calm like this mesa. Not complicated and piled with garbage like a big city."

Hugh cleared his throat. "Well I'm not from a big city. Our pizza is nice and flat in Nottingham. In fact, I think they made a proclamation some time ago, ensuring that no pizza is taller than one half inch. They have designated pizza inspectors, just to make sure." Hugh's sarcasm was thick. It surprised Violet how he stood up to the lawman.

The sheriff didn't flinch. "There's actually three things I hate. The third is pompous educated types who think they know more than a dumb ol' small town sheriff. That would be a mistake, wouldn't it Jones?" The deputy nodded his head somberly.

"Mundi Madness is very important to this county," the sheriff said, staring them down. "I'm not happy this year's festival is tainted by a murder investigation. So I'm gonna do my best to move things along. You're not going back to town until Jones here gets a full statement. I'll be questioning you later." He began to walk quickly back to his truck and then turned around.

"One more thing, Professor. Don't get any ideas about sailing back to Merry Old England. You and the Deep Dish are gonna spend some time with us here in Coatimundi. You don't leave this county. Got it?" He didn't wait for an answer. Violet and Hugh watched as he climbed into his sheriff's truck and drove off.

CHAPTER 6

"I am so, so sorry," Violet said, from the passenger seat of the old green pickup. Hugh was driving this time because Violet felt too shaken up to take the wheel.

"There are no victims, only volunteers," he said, with a bit of humor in his voice. "I'm not totally sure what that means, but that's something we therapists are supposed to say. In this case, it's true. I came along with you voluntarily for—for my own reasons. And the outcome was completely out of your control."

Violet silently wondered about Hugh's reasons. He said he was bored and ready for a change. But was that enough to pick up and join her in her quest to find Jim? Now he was caught up with her in this mess. She had to make sure he was cleared as soon as possible, so he could get back to his own life.

"Thank you for that, you always know the right thing to say," she said. "But there *is* a victim in this case—Jim. And that Sheriff thinks you and me are at the top of the suspect list."

"Yes, he did seem like he's in a hurry to wrap

things up so he can get back to his Mundi Madness."

"I know what we have to do," Violet said suddenly.

Hugh cocked an eyebrow. "Jump in the RV and head for Mexico?"

"No—although that's tempting. We have to figure out who killed Jim."

Hugh was thoughtful for a moment. "I don't know about here, but in England, the authorities don't take very kindly to people interfering in a murder investigation."

"I don't think we have much choice. And I know right where to start. Did you see those women's underthings at Jim's place? On the clothesline?"

Hugh shook his head. "I must have missed that. I was trying to fend off coatimundi."

"Anyway," Violet continued, "He must have had a woman staying there with him. Where is she? *Who* is she? I know from experience that living with Jim can drive a woman crazy."

"But that doesn't explain the place being turned upside down," Hugh said. "I'm leaning toward that group from Chicago. They had a motive—Jim stole money from their disabled mom."

As they pulled into the RV park, they could see the sheriff's truck out front. Sheriff Winters was standing outside Room 7 and appeared to be questioning the group from Chicago.

"That's a good sign," said Hugh, "It looks like the sheriff is getting to work."

Violet looked at the group thoughtfully as they

drove past. She didn't think they had anything to do with Jim's death. If they had found Jim, ransacked his place and killed him, they would have gotten out of town. Unless they didn't find what they were looking for. I'll put them toward the top of the list of people to question, she thought, before they leave town.

Violet and Hugh went to their respective RVs to rest and eat. She lay down on her bed and closed her eyes. So Jim was dead. She felt devoid of any feeling about his demise, despite his gruesome end. Did that make her a bad person? Should she feel sad about his death? She just felt empty. She allowed herself to think back to when they were first dating. He was very confident and brash and in those days he could be quite generous. That went away as soon as they were married. In fact, he shouted at her on their wedding night, accusing her of flirting with a waiter.

Violet had wanted her share of the house— needed it. It was the nest egg she had intended to use to finance an escape from Chicago, to anywhere, to start a new life. But not enough to kill over. Someone else had obviously been burned by Jim—and that person wished him dead.

Sometime later she was awoken by a knock on the door. She hadn't meant to fall asleep and she was momentarily disoriented. The knock came again. She stumbled over to the door and opened it, expecting it to be Hugh. But it wasn't. An attractive, diminutive woman in a sharp navy suit stood staring back at her. Special Agent Montoya from the FBI. And she did not look pleased.

CHAPTER 7

Violet gaped at the agent, speechless. She hadn't expected to face the piercing glare of Montoya so soon.

"Are you going to invite me in, or—?" The FBI agent left the rest unsaid, but Violet understood she meant *are you going to make me stand out here all day?* From Violet's previous dealings with Montoya, she knew underneath the polished, polite FBI front was a tough, street smart woman. She formerly worked as a Chicago homicide detective, a fact the agent had mentioned herself upon their first meeting.

"Don't look so surprised, Mrs. Vaughn. You had to realize we'd be out here eventually. Locating a middle-aged thrift-store worker driving the world's slowest RV wasn't that difficult. You're not exactly a brilliant criminal mind. And that's a good thing." She didn't wait for an invitation and climbed up the short step and inside. Her sharp eyes did a sweep, taking in the sparse surroundings and Violet's added flairs of style.

"Have a seat," the agent ordered, pointing to the little dining area with bench seating. Violet did as she was told and Montoya sat down opposite. Violet noticed not a dark, shiny hair was out of place in her sleek bun and not a speck of dust showed on her navy suit. Her white shirt was creaseless—even wrinkles seemed afraid to defy Montoya. What she lacked in stature, she made up for in attitude.

"You weren't supposed to leave the Chicago area. I thought I made that clear."

Violet made a little strangled sound in her throat, trying to come up with an excuse.

The agent put her hand in the air, stopping her. "It doesn't matter now. We were already on the trail of Jim Vaughn, but your little escapade allowed us to focus in on his location. And now—" Her eyes met Violet's and they were blazing. "Two years," she said. "That's how long I've been investigating Vaughn. For those two years, every day I pictured myself putting cuffs on him and getting some justice for his victims. Someone cheated me out of that."

"It wasn't me," said Violet quickly. "Please believe me. I just wanted to face him and find out about the money from the sale of my house. But he was dead when I found him. And by the way, I manage four second hand boutiques—I'm not a thrift store worker. Not that there's anything wrong with that, I've been one of those too."

The agent reached into her jacket and pulled out a white envelope. "Since I can't lock him up, I'm putting all our efforts into finding that money. We've long suspected Vaughn had a ton of cash. We're pretty sure he brought it out here with him. You're going to help me find it. Unless you already know where it is, which I doubt. Here—" She handed Violet the envelope. "This showed up at your apartment two days ago."

It was a letter, addressed to Violet in Jim's handwriting. "You opened my mail?" she said, looking the agent in the eye.

"We had a warrant, ma'am. We searched your whole apartment. You don't have much to hide, Mrs. Vaughn, which makes me wonder why you're messed up in this. I encourage you to be forthcoming with me from here on out." Violet interpreted the agent's encouragement as *don't lie to me.*

The agent met her gaze and didn't blink. "Read it," she said. "Out loud."

Violet opened the letter and drew out a single sheet of unlined paper, covered in Jim's messy scrawl. "Dear Vi," she read. "Sorry about the house. I'm sure you know about it by now. It was never my plan to do that to you, but things were closing in on me and I had to leave quickly. You probably know about the other stuff too. The feds will be poking around. Don't come looking for me. A lot of people want me dead. You won't be sad to hear that, I'm sure. I wasn't a good husband, I know that. But I still think of you as my wife, I always have. You're the only one I really care about. Now listen. Remember that place I told you about a long time ago? The place I said I would go? I have something for you there. To find it, you just have to remember what I told you. Don't go looking for it unless I'm dead and gone awhile. There's vultures everywhere. Jim."

Montoya looked at her expectantly. "So?"

"So what?"

"What's he talking about? What did he tell you about where he hid the money?"

"Nothing," said Violet, shaking her head. "He told me about this place, Coatimundi, that he bought land out here, but that's all I remember. And this letter proves I didn't kill him! He says people wanted him dead."

The agent gazed at her intently, looking like she was reading Violet's very soul. Finally, she got up and said, "Let's go. You're coming with me."

"Are you arresting me?" Violet cried.

"Should I?" The agent glared at her. "No. Not today. I need to go see the crime scene. Maybe being out there will jog your memory. I want to get that money back for his victims. Come on, we're heading out to your husband's place.

From the passenger seat of Montoya's SUV, Violet sent a text to Hugh giving him a quick summary of events and where she was. She knew he would be worried if she just disappeared. She glanced over at the agent. As tough as she appeared, Violet had a grudging respect for her. The woman was a good twenty years younger than herself and yet she seemed to be in complete control. She drove, talked on her earpiece phone and easily followed the coordinates programmed into the GPS. She exuded confidence.

A squad car blocked the turnoff that led to Jim's trailer. The agent flashed her badge and drove on through. They approached a completely different scene than the first time Violet came down this road. Was that only this morning? It seemed like ages ago. Vehicles were everywhere. A mobile crime lab dominated the area, shiny and clinical. Forensic specialists dressed in white jumpsuits moved around busily.

"I doubt Sheriff Winters would be pleased to see me wandering around out here," Violet said as they got out of the SUV.

"Don't wander around. Stay back here by my vehicle. Try to think of what your husband told you. It may have been a long time ago, but it's my only lead right now. Any detail might help."

Violet stared after the small woman who strode briskly up the road. Then she wandered away from the car and into the brush. She sat down on a rock and pulled a granola bar out of her purse. It was a little mashed, but she was grateful to have it. She looked at the scene spread out before her. The rain earlier in the day enhanced the desert, bringing out the clean smell of sage and making the colors more vibrant. The beauty wasn't enough to wash away the sick sense she had looking at the place. Jim's place—where someone killed him.

She closed her eyes and breathed, taking her mind back to the time long ago when Jim told her about Coatimundi.

They were sitting on the sofa in their first

apartment, eating take out and watching the news when a story came on about a missing man.

"He probably flew the coop," Jim said.

"What does that mean?"

"You know, did a runner. Disappeared himself." Violet still didn't get it.

"You're so naïve, Vi," he scoffed. "Did you see his wife? What a battle ax. That guy started over somewhere, mark my words." He shook his head. Jim always thought he was smarter than everyone. Maybe the so-called battle ax was married to someone like Jim and had his body hidden in the cellar, she thought at the time.

"You know, I'm gonna tell you a secret. I have a place, if I ever need to disappear."

"Why would you need to disappear?" she asked, alarmed.

He shrugged. "Who knows? When I was rolling around the country after college, I just happened to stop in this bar and had a drink next to a guy who needed some money. Owned a big ranch in the middle of nowhere—but he was strapped. He said he'd sell me a little piece of it for cheap, said it used to be a watering hole for horses. He drove me out there and that's all it was. An old windmill at the base of a hill and a bunch of nothin. But I thought, if I ever needed to get away, no one would ever find me out there. Place is called Coatimundi."

Now Violet gazed at the scene before her. How was she supposed to get anything out of that? What else was there? The story about the guy in the bar?

But that wouldn't provide any clues to where money was hidden. She looked across the open space to see Montoya talking to a group of men. The agent was at ease and in her element. They must be other FBI agents, talking shop.

An enormous sense of loneliness overtook Violet in that moment. She thought she had gotten away from Jim ten years ago, but had she really? For all these years she remained tethered to him, emotionally and legally. It was an excuse to put distance between herself and others. She had let it go on too long. Just putting one foot in front of the other, days turned into weeks turned into years. She didn't have any close relationships, not even friends.

She saw Montoya heading back. She would need to come up with something to tell her. Her hopes of realizing any money from Jim were now secondary to exonerating herself and Hugh.

Now the agent was standing in front of her looking down at her with an eyebrow cocked.

"So?"

"I thought of a couple little things, but first— what's going on with the investigation to the murder? Do they know who killed him?"

"I can't say right now."

Violet didn't know if she meant she didn't know or couldn't reveal what she knew. She wasn't giving anything away, that's for sure.

Violet relayed what she recalled about the rancher who sold Jim the property and that it used to be a watering hole. The agent immediately dialed her phone and spoke into her headpiece.

"Get me info on the former property owners. And look near the windmill as a potential dig site, maybe an old trough or container. Okay, let me know."

Back in the car, they drove in silence for a few minutes and then, up ahead, Violet saw something at the side of the road. As they came closer, she could see it was a dog. A very skinny, dirty dog, limping slowly down the road. Montoya saw it too.

"Oh hell no," she said. She pulled the car to the shoulder and jumped out. Violet followed at a distance, not knowing if the dog was aggressive.

"Hey, pup," the agent said in a soothing voice that surprised Violet. "Hey little pup, it's okay, I'm not gonna hurt you." The dog turned luminous sad eyes on Montoya and collapsed at her feet. Violet moved forward, knelt down and patted the dog's side.

"You think he got hit by a car?" she asked the agent.

"No. I grew up in a desert just like this. People dump their animals out here. Throw them out like trash." She looked around in anger, as if the perpetrator might be nearby, and heaven help them if they were.

"Border collie." She said. "They're great dogs, hard workers, loyal." She stroked the dog's head. "We need to find a vet."

They heard a vehicle approaching and they looked up to see a pickup truck bouncing down the road. It pulled over and an older man with a gray beard called out.

"You alright, need some help?"

"Where's the closest vet?" said Montoya.

"Well that's the Navajo Nation vet clinic. But I saw Dr. Wauneka's truck over at the Perry ranch. It's vaccination day for the sheep. If you hurry you might catch him."

Violet got directions while the agent picked the dog up in her arms and placed him on the back seat. She opened a bottle of water and poured a bit into the dog's mouth, then they followed the man's directions to the ranch.

The Perry ranch was a busy place, but the first person they asked pointed them to a white Ford Bronco that had "Navajo Nation Veterinary Clinic" stenciled on the side. Dr. Wauneka was just packing up to leave. He was a large Native American man in his forties with black and silver hair and a kind, handsome face. He wore jeans, a plaid shirt and a turquoise belt buckle.

Violet waved him down. "Doctor, can you help us?"

Montoya approached with the dog in her arms. Dr. Wauneka grabbed a thick blanket out of his truck, placed it on the ground and motioned for the agent to set the animal down. He knelt and began an examination.

"Looks like we have a young male border collie. He's pretty banged up. We see a lot of abandoned animals." He shook his head. "All people have to do is drive a few miles to the animal shelter, but they don't. Maybe they're ashamed. Who knows?" He looked at

Violet and the agent and seemed to take them in for the first time. "You new to town? Or here for the festival?"

"I'm Special Agent Montoya, FBI, here working on a case. And this is Violet Vaughn."

His eyebrows shot up. "You're the one with the, uh—husband." Although there were a lot of husbands in these parts, Violet knew what he was talking about.

"Estranged husband," she said.

"Deceased husband," Montoya added.

"Yeah, him," said Dr. Wauneka, continuing to examine the injured dog.

"How did you know about that already?" asked Violet.

"I know pretty much everybody on this mesa that has an animal and I've already been to a bunch of ranches today. It'll be halfway around the county by now and all the way around by tomorrow."

"Did you know the deceased? Jim Vaughn?" prodded Montoya.

"Him? No," said the doctor as he inspected the dog's paws. There followed a silence where Violet suspected the doctor might know more than he was saying. She figured Montoya wouldn't let it go. She was right.

"So you didn't know him, but? What aren't you saying doctor?"

"No, I didn't know him. But I know—" he glanced at Violet. "His, um—lady friend."

Montoya knelt so she was on the vet's level. "And?"

"Her name's Jennifer Norris. Born and raised here in Coatimundi. She's one of those that was always trying to get out of this town. Works in some business on Main Street. She has a little Chihuahua named Princess. That's all I know. So am I free to go now?" he said with a chuckle.

"No," said Montoya. "Not until you tell us about this dog. And thank you for the information, doctor. I may need to follow up with you later."

Doctor Wauneka stroked the dog's side and was thoughtful for a few moments. "This dog has probably been surviving on his own for a few months. He's dehydrated and his paws are torn up. He's damn lucky the coyotes didn't get him. Some ranchers would likely put him down."

As if knowing they were talking about him, the dog turned his head and licked the vet's hand. Dr. Wauneka patted his side.

"But I think you have a nice dog here. He has good spirit. Who's taking responsibility for him?"

"I am," said Violet. She said it without thinking, but as soon as she said it, she knew it was right. She wanted this dog. Montoya gave her a look that in a very tiny way appeared grateful.

"Okay," said the doctor. "I'll take him back to my clinic in White Feather. That's in the Navajo Nation, about ten miles from here. I'll get him some fluids and some rest, fix him up a little. We'll check to see if he's microchipped. Call me in a few days." He scooped the dog up and put him in the Bronco. Violet reached in and gave the dog one last pat on the head.

"Looks like it's gonna be you and me, buddy," she said and then thought to herself—if I'm not arrested for murder.

Violet saw the FBI agent was standing next to her car, talking on the phone again. When they were back on the road, the agent shook her head. "This case keeps getting weirder and weirder. You'd think working homicide in Chicago I would have seen it all, but this is a special kind of crazy. We have a town in the middle of nowhere with a name no one can pronounce, a hidden treasure, a dead guy, a tie-dye wearing sheriff and now added to the mix we've got one of Great Britain's leading forensic psychologists."

Violet looked at Montoya, confused. "Wait—what? Who?"

"You know, your boyfriend," said the agent. "Dr. Hugh Gordon."

CHAPTER 8

"This time when I say don't leave town, I mean it," said Montoya as they pulled up to Maven's. "And I have the pleasure of staying right here in this little piece of heaven since apparently it's the only motel in town, so—I'm watching you."

Violet nodded, but she was barely listening. She was so full of hurt and anger about Hugh she could barely think. He lied to me, she thought. Why? As she walked the path toward her RV, she saw Hugh standing outside, giving her a wave. She veered off and picked up her pace, walking into the surrounding desert.

"Hey!" he called. "Vi! What's wrong?" He was following her now, calling after her.

"Don't call me Vi!" she yelled behind her. "And leave me alone!"

"What's happened?" he said, getting closer.

She kept walking, making her way through sage and cactus. "You tell me, Mister Robinhood from Nottingham Forest! Mister sweater vest wearing mild-mannered therapist!"

"Violet, stop!" he called. She kept going.

"Stop!"

She felt herself grabbed in a bear hug from behind and forced to a standstill. She began to struggle, but then she heard it. Although she'd never heard the sound before in real life, she instinctively knew what it was. She froze and slowly lifted her head. About five feet in front of her was a large rattlesnake, coiled and ready to strike.

"Don't. Move." Hugh whispered in her ear. His arms were strong around her. They stood stock still, facing off with the snake. The rattle sizzled in the air while the agitated reptile stared them down, it's black, forked tongue flicking in and out.

"We're gonna back up," Hugh whispered. "Slowly."

She felt him taking a very slow step backward and she moved with him. One slow step, two. Then Hugh released her, grabbed her hand and said, "Run!"

Hand in hand they bounded over the brush, not stopping until they reached Hugh's RV where they clasped each other in a hug.

"Are you okay?" said Hugh.

"Yes," she breathed out, her head on his chest. Then coming to her senses, she put her hands on his chest and pushed him back. "I mean no. I'm not okay. You lied to me."

"I didn't lie to you. I don't know what you've heard, but I think you at least owe me the benefit of the doubt. Hear me out, Violet." He gestured toward his RV and it was then that she noticed what he had done. Evening was setting in and Hugh's outdoor lights were strung up around the awning. A fire crackled in the fire pit. Next to that was a small table covered with a white tablecloth. There was a bottle of wine and a large spread of tasty-looking hors d-oeuvres.

"I've said it before—you always know the right thing to say." Violet walked quickly toward the table. "This time you said it to my stomach and I've had a grand total of one smashed granola bar today." She sat down in a chair and picked up a hunk of cheese. "I'm all ears."

"Just eat something," he said, coming to sit down beside her. "Breathe for a second. It's not every day you find your husband dead, get picked up by the FBI and have a near miss with a rattlesnake."

"And rescue a dog," she added. "I'll tell you about that part later. Right now I want to hear about Dr. Hugh Gordon, forensic psychologist. Why weren't you honest with me from the beginning?"

Hugh sighed. "Alright. First off, I didn't lie. I am a therapist. I retired from forensic psychology a few years ago. I still write books and do some expert witness stuff, that's about it."

"Oh, is that all?" said Violet, her voice full of sarcasm. "So why did you come with me? Am I some kind of project for you, some kind of guinea pig for your book?"

Her voice came out a lot snarkier than she intended. It must be this horrendous day. Then it dawned on her. He didn't owe her anything. In fact, she owed him. Big time. She really was out of practice with this friend thing, if she ever had been in practice in the first place. She took a deep breath and forced an attitude adjustment.

"I'm sorry."

"Don't be," he said. "And no, you're not a project for my book. But I will admit you did start out as a personal project. Or maybe a project for personal redemption."

"That sounds intriguing. Go on."

"When you rolled into that campground in Missouri, I was at an all-time low. My wife left me for my best friend, I dropped my only child off at college and I was wandering around America alone on the trip I was supposed to be on with my wife." He paused in his story and poured some wine for himself. Violet continued to gorge on the snacks as if she hadn't eaten in weeks. She felt herself coming alive again and was feeling much less angry at Hugh. He sat back in his chair and continued.

"At the same time I was reviewing material from some of my past cases for my latest book. Some really depraved individuals. I was in a really dark place."

Violet felt a little squeeze on her heart. She didn't like thinking of Hugh being sad. She popped more cheese in her mouth.

"When I met you and heard your story, I smelled trouble," he went on. "Not intuition, just years of experience. I knew something awful was going to happen with that Jim character and I was worried for your safety. For once I found myself in the position of being able to prevent something bad, to protect someone before the fact. Not to mention embark on an adventure that would get me out of my rut. A lot of good it did though. Jim's dead and we're both suspects in a murder." He held up the wine glass. "This stuff isn't too bad. Mundi Mini Mart's finest vintage."

Violet smiled. "So what's this forensic psychology stuff all about? Profiling serial killers?

"Hardly. There were only a few of those in my entire career. The rest is just figuring out your average bad guy. And I'm not sure if I even made much progress there." They both sat in silence for awhile, enjoying the fire, food and wine.

Finally, Violet looked at Hugh. "Thank you. For everything. I had no right to question you. I was just—shocked. Here I thought you were the warm and fuzzy, Birkenstock-wearing counselor type, and instead you've spent most of your life dealing with criminals."

"I'm sorry to have misled you." He reached across the table to take her hand. "And I assure you, I am very warm and—"

"Hello! Hey there!" Maven emerged from out of the darkness, followed by her partner Maddie. "Hope we're not interrupting."

Violet and Hugh, startled, sat up straight in their chairs. "No, not at all," Hugh said, although not convincingly. He seemed to shake it off though and went into host mode. "Welcome," he said, "won't you join us?"

"Don't mind if we do," said Maven, striding over. Hugh jumped up, grabbed some folding chairs and arranged them next to the fire. Violet found some cups and poured wine. When everyone was settled, Maven said, "Well. We just had to come over and find out what's going on. It's the talk of Coatimundi. It's even bigger than Mundi Madness!"

Violet had a feeling that not much in Maven's world was bigger than Mundi Madness, so there was no telling what sort of stories the rumor mill was kicking out. She also had a bad feeling about the festival being eclipsed. That was the exact thing Sheriff Winters said he didn't want to happen.

"I guess you probably know we weren't completely honest when we got here, and I'm sorry for that," said Violet. "It's a long story, but I want to assure you, we had nothing to do with the murder of Jim Vaughn."

"Oh we know you didn't," said Maddie. "And we have proof."

CHAPTER 9

Violet sat forward with such force she nearly fell out of her chair. "Really? What proof?"

"Not so fast," said Maven. She lounged back in her chair and took a long drink from the wine-filled paper cup. Her long legs stretched out in front of her, cowboy boots peeking out underneath a long loose hippie skirt. Pink haired Maddie sat next to her with bright eyes and a grin.

"You two look like the cat that ate the canary," said Hugh, "but don't keep us in suspense. Sheriff Winters is licking his chops and Violet and I are the proverbial canary."

"First, I need some dirt," said Maven. "Tell me everything you know."

Violet didn't feel like sharing the details of her humiliation. On the other hand, the rumor mill was already cranking and gaining steam. It was probably best to get her own version of events out there. From what she knew of Maven so far, she could be counted on to pass the story along.

So Violet told them how she had come looking

for Jim, how he stole some peoples' money, including hers, and how she and Hugh found him dead in his trailer. She didn't mention her involvement with Montoya's search for the money. The last thing they needed was a bunch of people trying to find Jim's hidden treasure themselves. Maven leaned forward, avid to learn the gruesome details of the knife sticking out of Jim's chest. When Violet disclosed that Jim died with his boots on, Maven slapped her leg and let out a whoop.

"Oh Lordy, this is even juicier than I thought!"

Violet supposed Maven would tell this story, with her own embellishments, for years to come.

Hugh stood up and put a log on the fire pit. "Now please dear ladies, if you will—tell us what you know."

"We know you never left our property the night of the murder" said Maddie. We have a security camera pointing at the parking lot. The truck you rented from us never moved."

Violet felt light-headed as relief washed over her. The tension of the past twenty four hours was draining out of her like air from a balloon.

"But there's more," said Maven, wiggling her eyebrows. "Someone did leave that night. Someone else who was interested in Jim Vaughn."

CLANG!

The four friends jumped at the ringing sound of metal hitting the ground nearby, followed by an "OOMPH!" They all jumped up and moved in various directions, trying to locate the source of the noise.

Violet ran to the back of Hugh's RV just in time to see a shadowy figure disappearing into the night.

"Hey!" she called. "Are you okay? What are you doing?" There was no answer. After her earlier encounter with the rattlesnake, Violet was not going to search around in the brush. She returned to the fire and told the others what she saw.

Hugh held some metal fire tools in his hand. "Whoever they were, they were practically on top of us—they knocked these over."

"Probably just someone who drank too much and couldn't find their trailer," said Maven. "Happens all the time."

"I don't know," said Violet, as she sat back down. "I'm totally paranoid right now. I'm ready to jump out of my skin. I have a feeling they were spying on us."

Hugh patted her shoulder. "You've had several scares today. You need some rest."

"Yes, I know, I really do. But I need to hear what they found on the video."

"Like I said, your truck didn't move," said Maddie. "But you know that group from Chicago, the family who brought the private investigator with them? We saw the P.I. leaving that night around eleven."

Violet and Hugh looked at each other, with jaws dropped.

"But get this," said Maven, leaning forward and speaking very slowly, lowering her voice to a mysterious whisper. "He never came back to his room. The family says they think he headed back to

Chicago."

"Have you told all this to the authorities?" asked Hugh.

"Of course," said Maven. "We called Sheriff Winters right away. I expect he'll get it all sorted out."

Violet didn't have the confidence in the sheriff that Maven and Maddie appeared to. But between the letter from Jim and this new evidence about the P.I., she felt much better about the chances for she and Hugh to get off the suspect list.

Hugh leaned back in his chair. "That makes me feel slightly better. I'm not sure what the jail looks like in your uh—quirky little town, but I'm not anxious to find out. Speaking of that, there's something else I've been wondering about. The coatimundi, the animal— can you tell us more about it?"

Maven glanced at her partner. "Maddie's the expert on all the little mesa critters."

Maddie's hand went up to touch a pin on her denim vest, a tiny silver coatimundi. "Oh, I love coatis, they're my spirit animal. They're really very interesting!"

Hugh laughed. "I can see I asked the right person. You said coati?"

"Yes, most people around here use the shortened name. The word coatimundi comes from the Tupi language spoken by indigenous people in South America. It comes from the words nose and belt because they tuck their nose into their tummy while they're sleeping."

"They almost look like a monkey or a lemur

with that tail," said Violet.

"Actually, they belong to the raccoon family. They use that long, fat tail for balance. They aren't nocturnal, like raccoons, but they are scavengers and will eat anything. They get into garbage cans, cars—"

"Trailers," put in Violet.

"Oh yeah, definitely, if a door is open, they'll go in. And it may be a lot of them because they live in bands of up to thirty."

"Why do you say it's your spirit animal?" asked Violet.

"In Mayan folklore, the coati was known as a prankster—a clown. They're even found on some ancient Mayan pottery." She reached up to fluff her short, pink hair. "I think it fits me."

As the conversation rolled on, Violet found it hard to keep her eyes open, despite the entertaining company. She wanted to review all the new information with Hugh, but right now she was too exhausted. The smell of wood fire and sage hung in the still evening air, making her even sleepier. She said goodnight and Hugh watched as she made it safely back to her RV.

Back inside, her mind felt too busy to sleep. She looked in the mirror and was shocked at her appearance. Her normally neat and smooth bob looked more like a black rag mop. She reached up and picked off a piece of sage brush. She had mascara under her eyes and the silk scarf she artfully tied around her neck this morning hung dirty and lank.

Winnie the RV actually had a bath tub of sorts.

It was half the size of a normal bath, but at that moment, it looked heavenly. She indulged in a face mask and bath then pulled on her silk pajamas and snuggled into her cozy RV bed. She thought about the events of the day. The desert is breathtakingly beautiful and deadly at the same time, she thought. She wondered about the dog, hoping he was okay. I think I could get used to spending time in Coatimundi she mused dreamily. Minus the murder stuff. And then she fell into a deep sleep.

She awoke to the sounds of bustling activity outside. She could hear vehicles moving, voices shouting and laughter. She sat up and peeked out the curtains. RVs and trailers were pulling into the park. People milled about everywhere. A young woman rode past on a bicycle covered in pink fur and glitter. Mundi Madness had begun.

Violet brewed some coffee and dressed in a blue mohair sweater, jeans and boots. She added mascara and red lipstick for good measure—she needed to redeem herself for yesterday. Whatever she had to face, she would face it in style. Maven and Maddie's evidence was good, but it was circumstantial. Who knew what the Sheriff might think. And then there was Special Agent Montoya who wasn't too happy with her either. Still, things felt more promising today.

Outside, she didn't see any movement at Hugh's place, so she decided to walk around and check out the festival goers. People were setting up camp spots and rolling out awnings. Mundi Madness appeared to be an event that attracted not just artists, but free-spirits of all sorts. Many of the participants dressed in wild costumes, several involving body paint and glitter. Some worked on large art installations involving electrical wires and lights. There was a merry, laid-back feel and the atmosphere rubbed off on Violet. She found herself smiling and enjoying the morning, for the first time in weeks.

She reached the parking lot in front of the motel and saw a small group gathered. The Chicago siblings. The woman in the group, large and angry-looking, spied Violet. Her face scrunched and twisted into an even angrier look, if that was possible. Her arm slowly raised and she pointed a long finger at Violet.

"You!" she cried.

Violet stopped in her tracks. She looked behind her, just in case she wasn't the You being singled out. Unfortunately, no one was there.

"I'm sorry, are you talking to me?" said Violet innocently.

"Of course I'm talking to you. Murderer." The woman marched toward Violet, trailed by her two siblings. "We were so close to finding that man and getting Mama's money. We wanted to see him pay for what he did. Now we'll probably never get the chance for either."

"You don't think getting stabbed to death was payment enough?" said Violet. "At any rate, I didn't do it. I came out here to get my own money. I'm in the same boat as you. By the way, that P.I. you hired has more explaining to do than me. Where was he at the time of the murder? Where is he now? And where were all of you for that matter"?"

"For your information, the P.I. was useless. He was charging us an arm and a leg, then he went and abandoned us. I would think Jim Vaughn's *wife* would be a more likely suspect."

A woman passed by walking her dog and stopped dead in her tracks. She swung around and met Violet's eyes. Violet had to take a step back, such was the venom in the woman's glare—it was like facing the rattlesnake. The attractive redhead wore a green velour tracksuit with a matching green leash for her Chihuahua. She had a youthful appearance, but on closer inspection, Violet put her nearer to her own age. Botox works wonders, Violet thought, she looks good. Except for the witchy look on her face.

"You're Violet Vaughn?" she hissed.

Oh brother, thought Violet, what now?

The woman pushed into the group, dragging her little dog so it had to scramble to keep up. "You killed my Jimmy!" she wailed. "You're gonna pay for what you did, you psycho!"

Violet stared at the deranged woman. "I'm sorry —who *are* you?"

"Who am *I*? I'm his girlfriend. We were living together. Until you killed him! Now I can't even go home, our trailer is a crime scene. And I can't stay with Mama, she's allergic to Princess. So I have to stay here, in this dump. I'm sure the whole town is laughing at me, Jennifer Norris, having to stay at Maven's place."

Violet watched as the woman went through the full range of emotions, from angry to sad to indignant. What a little actress, she thought. The Chicago siblings stood with their mouths agape, glued to this new development. Other onlookers also stopped to gawk.

"You seem to be forgetting something," Violet said finally, with as much dignity as she could muster. "I am Jim's wife. Or—widow. Although we were separated, we were still married. So that makes you —" All heads turned to look at Jennifer. Violet left her sentence hanging, allowing Jennifer and onlookers to supply their own tantalizing word to fill in the blank.

The venom returned to Jennifer's eyes. "He was going to marry me. Me!" Violet wondered what fine qualities of Jim's the woman was interested in, but she had a feeling it was more to do with his cash than his character.

Maven appeared at that moment. She didn't look pleased and Violet's cheeks flushed. She realized she and the group were making quite an embarrassing scene.

"Stop it, Jennifer," Maven said calmly. "He was a crook, headed for prison. You got off lucky. Now, you people move along. You're harshing my mellow. Mundi Madness is all about good vibes." She waved her fingers in the air and did a little dance. Violet shot her a grateful look and used that moment to make her exit.

So much for my better day, she thought. She hurried away. All she wanted was to get back to the RV so she could talk to Hugh. She couldn't believe she was angry with him yesterday. He was the one shining light in this whole mess.

She didn't want to go back the way she came and risk running into the siblings or Jennifer, so she went around to the back side of the office. She could see an overgrown path that ran behind the motel rooms. Let's see—rattlesnakes or being called a psycho murderer, she thought. Rattlesnakes it is.

She made her way down the path, passing behind the motel. Just beyond the rooms, the path led out into the open desert. The noises of Mundi Madness melted away, replaced by the chirps of birds and the rustle of a light breeze in the brittle sagebrush. Violet made her way through the pebbled sand, occasionally startled by a lizard running for cover. A tiny yellow and gray bird perched on the spiny ear of a cactus, pecking at the dried fruit on the tip.

Maybe she should get a book on local plants and birds. Wait, why did she have that thought? She wasn't on vacation. The only reason she was still here was because the authorities ordered her to stay. But she must admit, she felt a connection to this quiet place. Perhaps the desolate landscape matched the lonely wasteland her personal life had become these past years. She yanked her thoughts back to the present. Ugh, don't go down that road. Geez, I need to schedule a therapy session with Hugh, she thought wryly.

Something caught her eye, lying in the sand at the base of a long-limbed, bush-like cactus. It was a small spiral bound notebook. She picked it up and examined it. The black, palm-sized notepad had not been outside for long and appeared crisp and new. The first few pages had a series of numbers. She flipped past those. There were some scribbled notes with numbers combined with letters that didn't appear to make sense and the word RED circled. She decided to hang onto it and give it to Maven.

She glanced up at the clear sky and noticed some unusual birds. Those are some very big birds, she thought, wishing once again for a bird book. There were three of them circling. Were those—vultures? She remembered Jim's words. *There are vultures everywhere.*

A rock formation nearby seemed like a good place to get a better look. She had never seen vultures before and wondered what they were circling. Maybe a steer skull and tumbleweeds, like in an old western, she thought, chuckling to herself. She made it to the outcropping of rocks, and climbed to a flat, elevated spot.

She had a good view of the open desert. Some taller cacti thrust themselves up between brush and clusters of rocks. Violet thought they looked like people in a hold-up, their arms raised high in the air. She looked for the vultures and then down at the ground, trying to see what they were circling. Then she saw it. She knew exactly what it was, or—who it was. A body lay sprawled on the ground, spread eagle, a vulture perched on his head.

The P.I. had not left town after all.

CHAPTER 10

"Okay, folks, everyone just calm down and have a seat. All of you." Sheriff Winters' jeans, shirt and hands were splattered with paint. Called away yet again from his precious float duties, Violet thought. A few hours had passed since she discovered the body of the P.I. and ran for help. Now, at the direction of the sheriff, Violet, Hugh and the Chicago siblings gathered in the small lobby of the motel. Through an awkward introduction, Violet learned the siblings were Jan Smart and her brothers Randy and Vince. The now-departed P.I. was named C.J. Denzer.

Violet and Hugh sat pressed together on a lime-green seventies print loveseat, jammed between two ancient metal racks full of travel brochures, postcards and road maps. Jan commandeered a garish cow-print wing-back chair. Randy and Vince's Chicago-sized bodies enveloped two teetering metal folding chairs.

Sheriff Winters put his hands on his hips and glared at his audience. "I've been sheriff here for twelve years. Every year for those twelve years we've had Mundi Madness. We have the occasional fight. We've had some drugs, some drunks. We have some people acting like fools. But mostly—it's good clean fun. And I'm proud of that."

The sheriff began to pace and looked each of the onlookers in the eye.

"But never—never have we had a murder. Let alone two."

"So you're saying the P.I. was murdered then?" Hugh interrupted. The sheriff glared at him.

"As I was saying, we've never had a murder. And now, this week, we have a group of outsiders—all from Chicago—who came here looking for another outsider from Chicago. With the exception of the professor here—" he pointed at Hugh. "Or should I say *doctor*, joining us from Sherwood Forest."

"Nottingham," Hugh interrupted again. "It's actually a fairly large city in the U.K. You might try googling it. Maybe you'll learn something."

"You can be certain I'm learning everything there is to know about you, Doctor Gordon, don't you worry."

"Perhaps you'll also learn that of the two and a half million people who live in Chicago, many of them are actually not murderers."

Hugh kept poking at the sheriff, so Violet decided to move things in another direction before he got in any more trouble. "Can you tell us how he died?" asked Violet. "How did he get all the way out there in the desert?"

"Maybe it was a Rattlesnake," Hugh put in.

Jan cranked her head around to look at Violet. "Or someone stabbed him."

"That information is part of our investigation and I'm not gonna disclose it to any of you," said Sheriff Winters.

"Just tell us what this is all about, why do *we* have to be here?" Jan glared pointedly at Violet again. "We all know who's to blame."

"It can't be me, if that's what you're suggesting," said Violet. "I never left this place on the night of Jim's murder. But that private investigator did. Maybe you all paid him to murder Jim. And then you killed the P.I. to shut him up."

Violet couldn't believe the words coming out of her mouth. Was she trapped in a bad TV crime drama? The door to the office opened. Agent Montoya stepped in and stood quietly next to the door, her face impassive.

"For that matter, what about Jennifer Norris?" said Hugh. "She was closer to Jim than any of us."

Everyone began to talk at once and voices rose. Sheriff Winters held up his hand and said, "Stop. I called y'all here to tell you not to leave the area. I'll be questioning each of you individually."

"But the security footage shows that neither Hugh nor I left on the night of Jim's murder," said Violet. "Why are we still suspects?"

"Who said you were a suspect?" said the sheriff. "But now that you mention it, I've seen the security footage. It's some pretty grainy video that shows a section of the parking lot. Here's a theory, Deep Dish. You walked up the road and met Mr. Denzer. You're both from Chicago, right? What a coincidence," he said, rubbing his chin. "You knew how to find your husband, but the P.I. didn't. You went and killed Mr. Vaughn and then you killed Denzer when you got back here. Then you and your boyfriend dragged him out to the desert and made him vulture food."

"Sheriff Winters," said agent Montoya. "This questioning is—irregular. These witnesses should be interviewed individually at the station. If you want to share your theories, you can share them with me and my team."

Sheriff Winters reddened and his eyes tightened into a squint. "Look, agent, um—Montoya. We have a certain way of handling things here that might be different than you're used to. But I assure you—I know what I'm doing."

"That's *special* agent Montoya. And I assure *you* —I'll be the judge of that. Go back to your rooms, folks. And stay close by. If you have any information that could be helpful, let us know." At that, she slipped back out the door.

"Let's get outta here," Hugh whispered to Violet. The two stood up to follow Montoya.

Sheriff Winters' face reddened into a deep plum and his voice sputtered out. "Wait, I haven't dismissed this meeting, hold on now—" But everyone was already up and pushing through the door.

Violet was eager to get away from the group and set a quick pace outside. Hugh took her arm and they began to walk toward the RV park.

"You know what I need right now?" said Violet.

"I can't even guess. Some way to erase ourselves

out of this Agatha Christie novel? I do love Agatha, but I prefer to be a reader, not a main character."

They strolled through the mostly-empty park. The Mundi Madness activities took place on the main street of Coatimundi. At this time of the afternoon, Violet figured things would likely be in full swing.

"I was thinking of a more immediate fix," said Violet. "Every time the sheriff calls me Deep Dish, I just start craving some deep dish pizza. Have you ever tried it?"

"I can't say I have. I've been to Italy and had some of the best pizza in the world, but I've never tried the Chicago style. By the way, why do you allow him to call you that? It's so insulting. Every time he says it, I want to slap him in the face."

"He thinks deep dish is an insult. But I don't mind, because I love deep dish pizza. And I need some right now. But I don't think we're gonna come across any around here. I make a mean deep dish pizza. I might be able to pull together some ingredients from the mini mart. If I could use your oven, I'll make us some. I need to decompress, and we need some time to talk about everything. It's all happening so fast." A rush of overwhelm washed over her and she felt a little dizzy with it. The quiet little life she was used had been completely upended.

Hugh held her arm a little firmer. "You poor thing, this is an awful lot to deal with in such a short time. Are you sure you wouldn't rather have me take you out to a nice dinner?"

"A nice dinner in Coatimundi?" she said with a

laugh. "Actually, I find cooking very relaxing."

"Well that's a coincidence, so do I," said Hugh, with his full-on British charm. "In that case—" Hugh spun them both around so they were once again headed toward the parking lot and exit. "Allow me to escort you to the Mundi Mini Mart, world-renown for its fine wine and gourmet food selection."

The feeling of overwhelm had passed, but Hugh's firm grasp on her arm remained. He's just being a gentleman, she thought, he would probably escort an elderly aunt in the same manner. She would not let his masculine proximity affect her. Much.

"A true Chicago-style deep dish is actually an upside-down pizza," said Violet. She rolled out dough at Hugh's bench-seat table, taking out aggression on the sticky, yeasty mound. Hugh stood at the stove and stirred a simmering red sauce. The rich smell of oregano and tomatoes filled the small space and warmed Violet's soul. Despite its compact size, Hugh's modern kitchen gleamed with small-scale amenities. It put Violet's kitchen back home to shame, from the stainless steel stovetop to the mini convection oven.

Hugh closed his eyes and took in a deep breath. "I think you are an amazingly smart woman. This is good therapy. So how is it upside down?"

"Hand me that pan and I'll show you." Violet lifted the round of dough and placed it on the cake pan Hugh handed her. She used her fingers to press the dough down on the bottom and up the sides of the pan.

"Cheese is next," she said.

"Really? Cheese on top of the dough?" He brought the bowl of cheese to the table. The mini mart didn't have a bag of mozzarella, so they improvised and shredded a bunch of string cheese sticks.

"Really. Like I said, it's upside down."

She poured the shredded cheese on top of the dough and spread it out.

"Pepperoni's next." She peeled the pepperoni out of its packet and layered it over the cheese.

"I'm starting to see the beauty of this," said Hugh. "It looks amazing."

Violet carried the pan up to the counter. "Now sauce."

She spooned the fragrant sauce over the top and smoothed it with a spoon. "All we have to do now is wait—which is gonna be tough, I'm starving." She put the pizza in the oven while Hugh poured out some hot tea.

"Some good strong English tea will tide you over. Have you tried real English tea?"

"No, this will be a first for me. I guess we're just a lesson in international cooperation," she said with a smile.

They both sat down at the bench seats across from one another and sipped their tea. Violet's thoughts returned to the pressing matter of the murders. In that moment she remembered the spiral notebook she found near C.J. Denzer's body. She reached into her purse and pulled it out.

"I know I probably should have given this to the

police. I found it on the path behind the motel."

Hugh flipped through the pages one at a time. "This is definitely Denzer's. Look at the top of the column—C.J.D hours. This first stuff looks like an accounting of his time and pay. And look at this—it appears the Smarts owed him $3,500. That could explain him going rogue."

"Or it could explain them killing him."

"Maybe," said Hugh. "But that's not much money to motivate a murder. Or was it murder? For all we know, he got drunk and stepped on a rattlesnake."

"What about the other stuff, the numbers and letters?"

Hugh perused the rest of the pages. "Well I know what this one means," he pointed at one of the scribbles. "It's my license plate."

"Of course!" cried Violet, "You're right! This one here is my license plate." They continued to look over the group of numbers.

"What do you think this RED means? Maybe a red vehicle?"

"Good thinking," said Hugh. "It's my hunch Mr. Denzer was on to something. He left that night to follow a lead. Whatever he saw, or learned—it cost him his life."

They sat silently for awhile and Violet pondered the gravity of the situation.

"It stands to reason, the person who killed Jim likely killed Denzer," said Hugh.

"It also stands to reason that the killer's license plate might be one of the ones written here," said

Violet. "Perhaps even a red vehicle."

"Now we're finally getting somewhere," said Hugh.

Violet sipped the English tea. It tasted very strong, almost like coffee. But it fortified her as Hugh had said it would. "I've been wondering. With your expertise, have you been able to build a profile of the murderer? Or murderers?"

"I don't have a lot to go on yet, but yes, I've been thinking about it—constantly actually. It's amazing how motivated I am to work when it's my own neck. First, I think we can rule out the P.I. as Jim's killer. It wouldn't make any sense—he needed Jim to be alive so he could get paid."

Violet nodded in agreement. "So we'll scratch him off the list. What else?"

"In this case, the murder weapon says a lot about the killer's mentality. Stabbing someone in the chest while they're asleep in bed is a very angry crime, full of passion. The ransacked house also speaks to desperation."

"So—someone close to Jim, who was angry and desperate—or desperate to find the money. That means the Smart family are still on the suspect list. They hated Jim and they're after the cash. But what about Jennifer Norris?"

"She fits the profile for Jim's murder, but not Denzer's. I can't see her overpowering him. At least not on her own."

The fragrant, spicy smell of pizza filled the air. Violet went to check it and found a bubbling, saucy masterpiece in the oven. "Oh yeah, it's done."

They took their pizza outside to eat under the awning. Violet cut into the deep dish and pulled out a slice as thick as apple pie. Long pieces of cheese stretched out from the pan with each piece she cut.

"Despite everything, I still managed to have a brilliant time tonight," said Hugh. "I really have been meaning to tell you—"

Footsteps crunched in the gravel near them. The strong beam of a flashlight found their faces and they were blinded.

A menacing drawl came from behind the flashlight.

"Well isn't this cozy."

CHAPTER 11

Violet didn't know if she should be relieved or frightened at the unmistakable voice of Sheriff Winters. He moved the flashlight away from their faces and Violet saw the gleam of his badge. For the first time since meeting the sheriff, he showed up in full uniform with khaki pants and a tan shirt. His police issue gun loomed on his hip and he had his hand placed lightly on it. Really, Violet thought, does he think we're that dangerous?

"Sorry to interrupt your little, uh—romantic dinner," the sheriff said with a smirk that showed he wasn't sorry at all. He walked closer to the table. Violet looked back and forth between the sheriff and her pizza. She hadn't even taken a bite yet. She vowed that if he was here to arrest her, she would grab her piece and eat until they put the cuffs on her.

"It's just a dinner between friends," she said, her voice coming out more relaxed than she felt. "And I made your favorite. Chicago-style deep dish pizza." She held up her slice. The sheriff backed away a bit and his nose crinkled. Apparently, deep dish pizza was his kryptonite. Or perhaps more like garlic for a vampire.

"If I could lock you up for—what should I call it —crimes against cuisine, I would. But as it happens, I'm here for another reason. I'm glad you two *friends* are sitting outside, because I got a warrant to search both of your places. So stay put. I'm also extending an invitation to come to the station tomorrow morning. We can have a nice chat about whatever we find tonight."

"Or whatever you don't find," said Hugh. "You're barking up the wrong RV, sheriff." Violet couldn't help sniggering at his little joke.

"We have nothing to hide," Hugh said. "So have at it. Cheerio, and all that."

Hugh concluded by taking a big bite of his pizza, the stretchy cheese strings as perfect as a TV commercial. The sheriff shook his head, disgusted, and turned on his heel.

Violet saw headlights of several cars pulling up. She thanked her lucky stars she had placed the spiral notebook in her back pocket before they came outside. She couldn't imagine what Sheriff Winters would think about her removing it from the crime scene and not turning it in. It would not look good if the police found it now. She knew she would have to turn it over, but she planned to give it to Special Agent Montoya, not the sheriff.

She took a big bite of her pizza and closed her eyes as she savored the rich blend of flavors. She opened them just in time to see Maven making her way toward them.

"Paddington Station," Hugh murmured under his breath.

Although she liked Maven, Violet was also becoming weary of the constant interruptions. But they needed the innkeeper on their side, so she forced a smile.

"I just *had* to pop in and find out what's going on." Maven put a hand on her chest, out of breath. "I heard about it in town and ran over here. Everything okay? So it's the sheriff, is it? Given a once-over to y'all's places?"

"Yes, it looks that way. I'm sure it's just routine," Violet added, remembering Maven owned the property and might be getting annoyed with their presence here. But Maven appeared more curious than bothered.

"Don't worry dear, they've been searching places all day. I'm not one of the ones who thinks you did it—no, not me. I'm a good judge of character, and I knew when I first met you folks that you were the good sort. Course, I've been wrong before, I've got three exes as prime examples." She let out a big hoot and slapped her leg a few times so that her turquoise bracelets jangled. "But I'm not wrong this time. What you got there?"

Violet held up her barely touched piece of pizza. "This? It's Chicago deep dish pizza. Would you like a slice?"

"Hell yes," said Maven, plopping down in a folding chair. "I've been at the festival all day. Lots of food down there, but it's all, you know, carnival food, like funnel cakes and such. And, I get a front row seat to the show." Her head swung around to take in the officers just entering Violet's RV. Violet handed her a slice of pizza on a paper plate. After taking one bite, Maven's brows shot up.

"Holy moly!" she exclaimed, slapping her leg again. "That's some good pizza! Not like any pizza I've tried before, I'll tell ya that."

Despite the interruption, Violet felt good about Maven stopping by after all. It was hard not to enjoy her company. And Violet felt a newfound thrill at having others enjoy her cooking.

"I agree," Hugh put in. He reached for the pan and cut himself another slice. "It's scrumptious." He winked at Violet and she felt herself blushing, something she hadn't done in many years. Some kind of nighttime songbird sang its heart out nearby. Violet wished again for a guidebook to local nature. And maybe for another kind of guidebook she didn't know the title of.

"Say, Maven," said Hugh, once he cut his slice. "You don't think we were involved in the murders. But I'll bet you have some ideas of your own. Who do you think did it?"

"Well now, that's a question." She leaned in and lowered her voice. "Between you and me—" She glanced over her shoulder. "They need to be looking a little closer to home."

"As in, Jennifer?" said Violet in a hushed voice.

"No way. That airhead has a leak in her think tank. Now you didn't hear it from me, but rumor has it your estranged husband had words with his neighbor. I guess things got pretty heated. Red Clayton's his name. He owns the big ranch out there. His daddy's the one that sold that piece of land to Jim."

Violet met Hugh's eyes. "You say the man's name is Red?"

"Yup. I'm runnin' my mouth again. Maddie says I need to quit that. I tell you,Violet, you could sell this pizza. I hope you don't mind if I eat and run, but I'd better get back to the festival." She hurried off as quickly as she came, taking her slice with her.

Violet's mind spun. "So, a red vehicle, or Red Clayton? That's the first we've heard that name mentioned."

"My blue-blooded nose smells affluence. It's the only thing that keeps cops away from a suspect. Did you notice Maven seemed wary of talking about it. And the way she hurried off? There's more to that story."

Violet watched the officers leave her RV. They didn't appear to be removing anything.

Hugh leaned forward and spoke quietly. "If we can get out of the cross-hairs for a minute, maybe we can pay a visit to this Red guy. We can try to find out if he's the RED in the P.I.s notebook."

"Yes, but whatever the P.I. was onto—it ended up killing him."

That thought forced her to grab another slice of deep dish. She made it a big one.

CHAPTER 12

The sheriff's office sat on the opposite end of town from Maven's Haven. That wasn't saying much, since the entire stretch of Main Street ran less than a quarter mile. The small, flat-roofed adobe building did not do much to shake off the Old West feel that Hugh always joked about. Small square windows flanked the wooden door, one with lettering that read simply SHERIFF. Violet sat outside on a wooden bench next to the door, waiting for Hugh and watching a tumbleweed blow across the street. The only thing missing from this place is a hitching post, she thought.

Down the main street, she could see festival venders setting up their stalls and tents. Coatimundi in the morning smelled sweet and earthy, like wet clay. She breathed it in and breathed out relief that her interview was over.

She had sat in an ancient wooden rolling chair pulled up to a desk in the front office, squeezed in close with Sheriff Winters and Deputy Jones. Stacks of paper and empty coffee cups littered the desk. A quick look around determined there weren't any interview rooms. She caught a glimpse of jail cells through an open door in the back and hoped wholeheartedly that she would never have to move further into place than the front room.

Deputy Jones brought her a bottle of water. The pleasant young man did not seem capable of the coldness and sarcasm displayed by Sheriff Winters. He endured numerous glares and pointed looks from the sheriff, but nothing stifled his affability. Violet retold her entire story, from discovering Jim sold the house from under her all the way to finding C.J. Denzer's body. The sheriff tried every way he could to trick her, but she stuck with her story and told the truth. The only thing she didn't mention was the spiral notebook. It seemed evident from the interview the sheriff was still eyeing her as a suspect. It seemed equally evident he didn't have a scrap of evidence. Hugh was inside now, giving his own version of the story.

She saw Jan Smart and her brothers Randy and Vince approaching. They seemed out of place, neither fitting in with the festival-goers nor the locals. Jan wore a knee-length black puffer coat, suitable for autumn in Chicago and her brothers wore Chicago Cubs jerseys and ball caps. Violet assumed they were here for questioning as well, which made her feel a little better.

"Oh, it's you," said Jan, as she reached the entrance. "I wish they'd lock you up so we can get out of this god-forsaken town."

"Nice to see you too, Jan," said Violet, rolling her eyes.

Jan reached for the door handle and then stopped. She turned back to Violet.

"Look. This isn't who I am. Maybe you didn't do it. And if you didn't, I apologize. I found out from that Agent Montoya that Jim did you wrong as well." She let go of the door handle. Her shoulders dropped and she appeared to crumple before Violet's eyes, the brazen confidence gone.

"Our mama was in a terrible accident and it wasn't her fault. She'll need care the rest of her life." Jan's voice caught and tears filled her eyes. "She needed that settlement money and we trusted Jim as her attorney. We came here to confront him and try to get our money—but we aren't killers. I just want to go home." The tears sprung out and rolled down her face. Violet was tempted to get up and give her a hug, but just then the door opened and Hugh came out. Seeing the Smarts, he held the door open while the ever-silent Randy and Vince guided Jan through the door.

"I leave you alone for a few minutes and you're making people cry," Hugh joked.
Violet opened her mouth to reply, but Hugh said, "Let's get out of here. You can tell me all about it on the walk back."

They made their way down the street, passing the quirky businesses and festival booths. It was still a little early for much action on the main street, but Coati Coffee was open and beckoned to Violet with its display of pastries in the window. They detoured into the shop and emerged a few minutes later, Violet with a cinnamon latte and a flakey apple turnover, Hugh an espresso and some kind of cream-filled wonder.

"I love that you love food," said Hugh.

"I really shouldn't be having this after all that pizza last night. At this rate, they'll have to roll me out of Coatimundi like a tumbleweed." She took a drink of the rich and sweet coffee. "But I'll worry about that later. Tell me about your interview."

"They've got nothing."

"Yeah, I had the same take. I think the only reason Sheriff Winters wants to pin it on us is because he just doesn't like us. And he hates Chicago. And deep dish pizza. Whoever actually did the murders was either very stealthy or very lucky."

"So what about Jan and the tears?"

"We had a bonding moment, of sorts. I really don't think they had anything to do with it. I feel bad for them, what Jim did."

They made their way through town and approached the motel.

"Should we find Red Clayton and pay him a visit?" asked Hugh.

"Yes, but there's something I need to do first. You want to get out of town for a couple hours? I need to see a man about a dog."

CHAPTER 13

The old green truck made its way up a gently-climbing mountain road, the curves hugging terracotta-colored peaks. Sand-blown rocks jutted out, painted by nature in an array of vibrant reds and oranges. They came around a curve into a flat desert spotted with low bushy trees and brush. A tall sign flanked by two boulders read "Welcome to the Navajo Nation."

"I'm so excited about this," said Hugh from the passenger seat. "I've been reading about the Navajo Nation ever since we got to the area. It's fascinating. You probably know all about it, having grown up in America."

"Actually, I know surprisingly little about it, so I'm as excited as you are. What have you found out so far?"

"The U.S. has other reservations and land areas that are held by different Native American tribes—but this is the biggest. It's bigger than ten of the states in the U.S., about the size of West Virginia. I don't know how big West Virginia is, my U.S. geography is a little sketchy."

"Don't worry, I doubt I could pick out Nottingham on a map."

They began to see some dwellings and a sign indicated they were entering White Feather.

"Oh look!" said Violet. She pointed at a long, brown, lodge-type building with a sign that said "Trading Post". Brightly-colored blankets and clothing hung from the eaves and pottery displays lined the front lot. "Let's check it out. Maybe I can find a book about local birds and plants."

Inside, they were met with the rich scent of leather and the grassy smell of baskets. The walls and shelves were filled with colorful goods of all sorts. Beautifully-woven blankets with Native American designs hung on the walls or lay in neat stacks on floor displays. Glass cases housed turquoise and silver jewelry. Rows and rows of shelves held artwork, handmade baskets, knick-knacks and books.

Hugh ran around like a little kid. He picked up a shopping basket and began filling it with various items. "Gifts for home," he said, and hurried off to explore.

In a book section, Violet found one about birds of New Mexico and one on local plants. She could easily spend thousands of dollars in the place. She would have loved to bring back a bunch of stuff to decorate her RV, but her meager funds would barely allow the two books.

She noticed a display of boots and moccasins. Her eyes landed on a pair of short boots near the front

—chocolate brown suede with a sturdy sole. They had a short fringe on the side and were lined in fluffy sheepskin. What really took her breath away was the beadwork on the toe of the boot. Purple, blue and green beads formed a flower resembling a violet.

"Oh, hello," she whispered to the boot, stroking the soft suede. Then she saw the price tag. "Goodbye, nice knowing you." Violet set the boot back down. Hugh was still off shopping. Well, maybe she could just try them on. She found her size and slipped her feet in. Of course, they were like butter. Pure bliss. She had gotten used to the pain of her high-heeled boots. She took a few steps and thought she might actually hear her toes sing.

"Now *those* are the boots for you," said Hugh, coming up behind her, his basket overflowing. "You shouldn't be suffering in those high-heeled things."

"Maybe some other time," said Violet, hurriedly taking them off and shoving them back in the box. "I guess we should get going, we need to find the vet."

A woman with short black hair and a Mundi Madness T-shirt stood behind the register. Her face reminded Violet of someone, but she couldn't put her finger on it.

"Do you know Dr. Wauneka?" Violet asked, as the woman rang up their purchases.

"Of course," she said with a smile.

"I guess everyone knows him, he's the vet," said Violet, feeling silly.

"Everyone does know him," she said. "But I know him especially well. I'm his twin sister, Grace."

Violet laughed. "I thought you looked familiar to me, you definitely resemble him. But prettier, of course. Then I guess you can help us with our next question. Where's the vet clinic?"

Grace gave them directions and wrapped their purchases. They headed back to the truck.

"Oh no, I left my phone inside," said Hugh, "I'll be right back."

White Feather appeared to be not much bigger than Coatimundi, and Violet determined they only needed to go a few blocks to find the clinic. Minutes later, Hugh got back in the truck. He held a large shoe box.

"Oh no you didn't," Violet said. "No, they're too much!"

"I don't want to hear another word about it." He sounded a little cross. "You need some better footwear. You can pay me back when you find Jim's treasure."

Violet was ashamed to admit she didn't need much arm twisting. She wasn't used to receiving gifts —and she loved the boots. "I'm going to put them on right now. And thank you. Very much. That was —very thoughtful of you." She felt herself getting emotional so she busied herself unwrapping the boots and putting them on. They felt even better knowing they belonged to her.

They found Dr. Wauneka's clinic, a square, flat-roofed place, sand-colored like most of the buildings in town. She gave her name to the receptionist, who, judging from her scrubs, also doubled as a vet tech.

"Oh, you're Spirit's mom," the young woman said excitedly. "Doctor wasn't sure you'd come. But I'm glad you did. He's such a good boy. The dog, I mean, not the doctor."

"I'm a good boy too, most of the time," said Dr. Wauneka. He stepped into the room, also wearing scrubs.

"Spirit?" said Violet.

"The vet techs started calling him that. But it fits. I'm glad you came."

Violet introduced Hugh and they followed the doctor into an exam room. In a moment, the vet tech came in with a dog in her arms. A bath and some rest had transformed the dog from the muddy mess they found on the road. Violet got a better sense of his markings now. His black and white fur looked silky, albeit a little patchy. A bandit-like black mask covered his face. His light blue eyes had been sad and fearful when she and Montoya found him. Now they twinkled, bright and friendly.

"Hello, Spirit," Violet said. Spirit's tail flopped on the table with a thwack thwack. He looked a little uncertain. So did Violet.

"You're not used to animals, are you?" asked Dr. Wauneka. "It's okay. Pet him. Let him know he's safe."

Hugh stepped up to the exam table and rustled the dog's fur. "Who's a good boy? Who's a good boy? Yes, he is," he said in a low voice. Spirit's tail began to wave wildly and he tried to jump off the table.

Violet stood frozen. This was a big mistake, she thought. She didn't know what she was doing or how to care for a dog. She tentatively reached up and gave Spirit's head a pat.

"He just needs more rest and a lot of good food," said the doctor. "But you can take him home. And don't worry about the fee. You did a good deed picking him up. He wouldn't have lasted much longer. Hang on, I have a couple of things laying around here to get you started."

Hugh had turned his attention to a bulletin board on the wall. A poster dominated one side. The artwork featured a close-up of a Native American woman, a red handprint covering the lower half of her face. Words in red print read: NO MORE STOLEN SISTERS.

A haunted feeling pierced Violet when she laid eyes on the poster. She dropped her hand to Spirit's side and gently stroked his fur. Dr. Wauneka returned carrying a cardboard box.

"Let's see, I found an old leash, a collar and half a bag of food. He'll probably sleep quite a bit for the next few days and drink a lot of water. You seem nervous, Mrs. Vaughn, but there's not much to it. He'll tell you what he needs. You said you had a connection with him when you first saw him. If you honor that, it will pay off in ways you can't imagine."

Violet's shoulders relaxed and she smiled at the doctor. He had such a calming manner. "Thank you so much. You're right, I do feel a connection. We've both—been through some things." Spirit's tail gave another thwack thwack at the sound of Violet's voice.

"We're going to check his weight one more time,

then you can go," said the doctor. The vet tech lifted Spirit off the table, took the leash and collar and left the room.

"Doctor, what does this poster mean?" asked Hugh.

A ghost passed over Dr. Wauneka's face. His good-natured calm evaporated in an instant.

"It's—it's about missing and murdered indigenous women. No More Stolen Sisters brings awareness about the murder rate. It's ten times the national average. For Native American women, the third leading cause of death is murder and many of the deaths go unsolved. My sister was one of them." The doctor sat down on the padded exam room bench.

"That's truly awful, doctor," said Hugh. "I hope I haven't upset you. That must be so painful for your family. We just met your twin sister Grace before we came here."

The mention of his twin brought a faint smile back to the doctor's face. "You must have been to the trading post. Yes, we're very close. Rainy's murder brought us even closer. It's okay to talk about it. I want as many people to know as possible. I got caught off guard for a moment. It happened last year, so I'm finding there are times lately when I'm not thinking about it. Then something will remind me again."

"You say your sister's murder is unsolved?" asked Violet.

"Yes. Jurisdictional problems play a large role in the number of unsolved cases. My little sister, Rainy, worked at a bar in Coatimundi while going to school.

She had to drive home late at night. One night she never made it back. They found her car along the highway, five miles outside of Coati. A few days later, they found her body on Navajo land."

"Isn't that Sheriff Winters' jurisdiction?" asked Hugh.

"They found the car in his jurisdiction. Three other women from White Feather have died in the past two years in the same way. But that guy's not gonna help us."

"You think it's like—some kind of serial killer?" said Violet.

"I don't know what name to put on it. I just know the women of White Feather are not safe."

"Doctor, with your permission, I'd like to look into this," said Hugh. "I'm a forensic psychologist and I have experience with this type of crime. Granted, my work has been in the U.K., but maybe I could be of some help. I might be able to find connections no one else has seen."

"That's kind of you to offer," said the doctor, "but don't you two have your own problems to deal with? The Bonnie and Clyde of Coatimundi?"

"That's the thing," said Hugh. "I'm rather stranded here at the moment, so I wouldn't mind looking into it. And as my friend Violet has pointed out, I'm a serial helper."

Dr. Wauneka agreed to email Hugh more details about the case and they left the clinic, Spirit in tow.

The addition of a dog made the cab of the truck

cozy. Spirit sat between Hugh and Violet. His head moved back and forth between them, following their conversation with his eyes bright and his head cocked.

"He really looks like he knows what we're saying," said Violet.

"Then I guess I should be saying 'the M word' instead of—you know."

"Murder?"

"That's the one."

"We've been saying that a lot lately, haven't we? What is it with this place? It's not all tie-dye shirts, peace and love, is it?"

Heading out of town, a painted sign with an arrow declared NAVAJO TACOS!

"Are you thinking what I'm thinking," said Hugh, now at the wheel.

"Definitely."

He made a hard right down a short dirt road that ended in a lot with a roadside stand. Violet clipped the leash on Spirit. As they exited the vehicle, they were met with the most exquisite aroma Violet had ever encountered. The tart, smoky smell came from a large barbecue grill completely covered with green peppers. A Native American man with tongs stood flipping them as they became black and charred.

"What kind of peppers are these?" Violet asked the pepper chef.

He cocked an eyebrow. "What kind of peppers are these? You're not from around here." It was a statement.

"Not even close," said Hugh. "They smell

delicious."

The man's eyebrow cocked even higher. "You're definitely not from around here. You sound like—Obi Wan Kenobi."

"These aren't the droids you're looking for," Hugh said, in a perfect imitation.

A smile lit the man's face. He placed two charred peppers on a red and white checked cardboard tray and handed them to Hugh. "Hatch chiles."

The buttery, tangy, smoky flavor was unlike anything Violet had ever tasted. Hugh bought several to take home, then they headed to a covered stand with a sign for Navajo tacos. These ended up being rounds of soft, pillowy bread piled with meat and traditional taco toppings. They sat on the bed of the pickup, savoring their meal and watching Spirit sniff around in the desert scrub.

The day with Hugh would have been perfect except for the murder investigation back in Coatimundi. It weighed on her constantly. She hoped it would be solved soon and they could go back to living their lives. But another thought niggled its way into her head. As soon as she and Hugh were cleared, Hugh would likely go on his way, returning to his tour of America. And she would—what? Go back to working in a thrift store in Chicago? Both thoughts were equally depressing.

CHAPTER 14

"So much for getting away from it all, we're back in Crazy-mundi," said Hugh. "And here's our welcoming committee."

A sheriff's car waited in the parking lot of Maven's Haven. A deputy paced next to it, talking to Montoya. Violet didn't recognize him, but from his wild gestures and head shaking, he appeared to be quite riled up. The young deputy's red hair shone like a bright flame on his head, which added to his fiery appearance. When they entered the parking lot, the deputy marched purposefully up to the truck.

As they opened their doors, he began calling out to them. "Mrs. Vaughn, Dr. Gordon, you aren't supposed to leave the area."

At that moment, Spirit jumped out of the truck and ran toward Agent Montoya with his tail wagging. She knelt down and rustled his fur. "Hello again," she said. Then she called out to the deputy. "It's all right. I'm—aware of this situation."

Violet saw the deputy's name badge. CLAYTON. "Are you related to Red Clayton?" she asked.

He raised his chin and attempted a haughty look, but with his boyish face he came off looking rather silly. "That's none of your concern. What *is* of concern is you people leaving town. We've been looking all over for you, thought you'd—absconded". He seemed to have been searching for the word, but was pleased with the one he landed on.

"We've cooperated with the sheriff up to this point," said Hugh, "but I don't think you can demand we stay in town. We're not under arrest."

"We just went into White Feather for a few hours," added Violet. "Was there something Sheriff Winters needed to tell us? Have they made any progress with the investigation?"

"No. He just don't want you to leave town. If I were you, I'd do as he says."

At that, he nodded at Montoya, climbed in his car and drove off.

"I feel like we're in another universe out here," Violet said.

Special Agent Montoya straightened up. "Rural sheriffs have to follow the law. But they do have some independence and I'm not the final word out here. There's some complicated things going on, Mrs. Vaughn. My gut tells me you're not involved, and I'm doing my best to keep this investigation clean. But I suggest you don't ruffle feathers."

Violet reached in her bag and pulled out the spiral notebook. "I found this in the desert out behind the motel. It might be important." Violet opened the notebook and showed the agent some of the things she and Hugh had noted.

"Thank you, this could be very important," said the agent. "But why didn't you just give it to Sheriff Winters?"

"He has it out for us," said Violet. "It's not even —rational."

"They're not used to having a double murder to solve. This is a big deal around here. In Chicago, this is just another day, but around here, they aren't equipped for this. Just stay under the radar."

"Do you have any idea how Denzer died?" asked Hugh.

"That information is already getting around town, you'll hear it soon enough. Shot in the back. With a shot gun."

"How horrible," said Violet, "That poor man."

Spirit pawed the agent's leg for a pet. "He looks good," she said, patting the dog's head.

"Dr. Wauneka's staff named him Spirit," said Violet. "I think the name fits. Speaking of Dr. Wauneka, there's another mystery going on. His sister was murdered last year. Several other Native American women have also died in similar circumstances. He says Sheriff Winters won't help. Hugh's going to look into it, but maybe you could—do something?"

"Mrs. Vaughn." The special agent let out a long breath and shook her head. "Don't you two have enough to worry about? Stay—" she looked from Violet to Hugh. "Out of it."

Violet opened her mouth to speak, but the agent

held up her hand. "I'll look into it. But you two—just don't." At that, she turned on her heel and headed toward the motel.

"She really wants us to mind our own business," said Hugh. "Trouble is, I still don't trust that sheriff. He wants the easiest way out."

"And that's us," said Violet.

"Right. I don't know about you, but I don't see any harm in paying a friendly visit to that Red Clayton and seeing what he's all about. After a nap."

"I agree with you. And yes, a nap sounds wonderful," said Violet. "Let's meet up in a few hours."

Inside her RV, Violet found a place to put some bowls on the floor and filled them with dog food and water. She set her old high-heeled boots next to the door and once again admired the cozy new ones on her feet. She removed them and lay down on the bed. Within a few minutes, she heard panting and felt like she was being watched. She sat up and found herself looking into the eyes of a dog staring at her, head cocked.

"Um—hello dog," said Violet. Spirit's head remained tilted in a dog question. Violet tried again. "Listen. I've never had a dog. I'm gonna do my best, but you have to help me out. You have to tell me what you need. It's you and me now. You and me."

Spirit's tail gave its thwack thwack on the floor and he dropped his chin on the edge of the bed. Violet patted the covers and said, "Come on up, I know you want to." It only took one pat for the dog to spring up on the bed, do a little circle and collapse next to her, his head nuzzling her leg. "See, we're communicating. That's a good start." She ruffled his fur.

At that moment, Violet noticed a stack of papers sitting on the bedside table—the home sale documents she took from Jim's trailer. She hadn't given them a second thought until that minute. She reached for them and then settled back against the pillows.

Several pages contained lines that required her signature. Violet's eyes grew wide at seeing a passable imitation of her own signed name. Stranger still, a notary's signature and seal appeared on the last page. A stamp revealed the name J.N. Brown. Who was this J.N. Brown? Some notary in the Chicago area? Had Jim shown up with another woman posing as herself? A quick search on her phone of J.N. Brown Chicago notary, turned up nothing.

There was one more page at the end of the documents. The words REAL ESTATE DEED appeared at the top. It appeared to be the property deed for Jim's land in Coatimundi. A blurry ink stamp at the bottom read SUNSET TITLE. Sunset Title? Violet remembered passing that business when she and Hugh walked to the barbecue restaurant. She made a mental note to pay them a visit.

Spirit let out a heavy, sleepy sigh next to her. Violet felt the same way. She closed her eyes and fell asleep within minutes.

CHAPTER 15

Violet and Hugh got directions to the Clayton ranch from Maven and Maddie. They bumped and rolled along the dirt road, passing Jim's property. Hugh slowed down and Violet saw that most of the police and forensic vehicles were gone from the property, replaced with an excavator and small bull dozer which were busy digging up dirt.

"Special Agent Montoya is pulling out all the stops," said Hugh.

"My understanding is Jim had his hands on millions of dollars in cash. They'll keep searching for a while, I'm sure. I just wish I knew what he meant in his letter. He seemed to think I knew what he was talking about."

"It's possible whoever killed him found the money and is now living it up in Mexico."

"True. But this is a very small town. Anyone missing would stand out."

They approached a cattle guard with an open gate. A modern metal sign read CLAYTON RANCH in fancy script. A smaller red sign read PRIVATE

PROPERTY. KEEP OUT.

"Let's leave the truck here and walk. If they're not happy with us, we can plead ignorance," said Hugh.

"You'd have to be pretty ignorant not to understand keep out. Let's just hope luck is on our side. Let's also watch out for rattlesnakes."

"I have a feeling Spirit will help us with that," said Hugh.

They ambled down the dirt road, past the cattle guard. Spirit ran here and there, chasing lizards. Soon, they came upon a field full of dusty white sheep. Further down the road, they could make out a large white-washed adobe structure, surrounded with trees and vegetation—a sparkling oasis in the midst of the scrubby desert. Spirit doubled back down the road and began to bark.

"Hold it right there!" The voice came from behind them and they froze. "Put your hands up and turn around slowly."

Violet and Hugh pivoted and found themselves staring down the barrel of a gun. Behind the gun, a tall red-haired man dressed in jeans, cowboy boots and a T shirt glared at them. The gun appeared massive to Violet and looked like what would probably be called a double-barrel shotgun. She didn't know anything about guns. But she didn't want to be facing this one. Spirit barked and growled at the man. Violet decided to take the offense and stepped forward.

"Hi. Hello there, sir. Sorry to intrude." Her voice wavered.

"What in the flying H am I lookin' at?" said the man. "Who are you people and what are you doing on my land?"

"So sorry, we can explain," said Hugh.

"Get to it, then. And call your dog off."

Violet called Spirit, who reluctantly came to sit next to her. "I'm Violet Vaughn and this is Dr. Hugh Gordon." She hoped that dropping *doctor* in there would give them credibility. "We're just looking for some information about, um—Jim Vaughn. You know, the man that was—"

"You're Mrs. Vaughn? Widow of Jim Vaughn?"

"Yes." Violet, inched closer to Hugh.

"Well hot damn, why didn't you say so?" He lowered the gun. "Mrs. Vaughn, I've been wanting to speak to you. I would say dying to speak to you, but that's probably not appropriate right now. You don't mind though, do you? You and he weren't close, that much I do know. Sorry about the welcome, but things have been crazy lately with murderers running around. I'm Red Clayton. Come on up to the house, I'll get you some drinks."

Momentarily speechless, adrenaline coursed through Violet's veins. She began to wonder if this was a trap. Why did he want to talk to her?

"No offense, old chap," said Hugh, "but how do we know you're not the murderer, luring us to our demise in the desert?"

"Well I didn't kill Jim. You'll just have to take my word for it if you want the information I have."

"Okay, we'll hear you out," said Violet. "Maven

knows we're out here."

"Maven? Tell that woman Captain Red Beard says hello," he said with a wink. "Now come on, I'll get you some drinks and some water for your dog."

The party continued down the road toward the adobe dwelling. As they got closer, Violet was awestruck by the veritable desert mansion appearing before them. Flowering vines cascaded over the walls and tiled paths ran up to the house. A red-haired teenage girl threw open a wrought iron gate in front and headed for the group. Violet marveled at the strength of the red-headed gene in this family.

"Daaad!" the girl wailed, stomping up the road. "The wifi is out again. Our coverage is so lame. Even kids in the *trailers* have better coverage than we do."

The girl seemed oblivious to the fact that her father had guests.

"I'll call about it later," said Red, "but I have company right now, pumpkin."

The girl rolled her eyes and stomped back to the house, slamming the gate behind her.

"My daughter, Bailey," said Red, the pride evident in his voice.

"Charming," said Hugh. Red beamed, the sarcasm sailing right over his auburn head.

"Is your son a sheriff's deputy?" asked Violet as Red ushered them through the wrought iron gate.

"Yeah, that's my oldest, Brody. He should be working out here at the ranch, but he always wanted to be a cop." Violet thought Red sounded a little bitter about this.

They found themselves in a lush and shady courtyard with a blue and white Mexican-tiled fountain in the center. Abundant terracotta pots overflowed with flowers and greenery.

Red strode ahead and Hugh whispered in Violet's ear, "The sheep business has been very good to him." She caught his meaning. This wasn't your average sheep farmer.

"You can leave your dog here. I'll have someone bring him some water."

They followed the rancher through double French doors and into a living room area. The inside of Red's home made the outside look positively provincial. The sofa and cushy arm chairs were rich brown leather. Southwestern art and textiles adorned the walls and shelves, including the type of Navajo blankets they saw in White Feather. A massive stone fireplace dominated the room. Over the fireplace hung a large Native American painting of what looked like a curved figure with a headdress, playing a flute. Violet walked over and gazed up at the striking piece of art.

"Kokopelli," said Red. "The deity of arrgriculture. He's supposed to chase away winter and bring about spring."

"It's almost—scary-looking," said Violet. The painting definitely gave her an unsettled feeling.

"Many of the Native American symbols are full of duality. They understand that with the light—comes darkness." Violet glanced at Red. For a moment she thought she caught a menacing look in his eyes. But seeing her gaze, he quickly pasted on a smile.

"What can I get you all to drink? Lemonade, tea —whiskey? I don't drink myself, but I've got a full bar, anything you want."

"Just water," said Hugh. Violet asked for the same. Red picked up a phone and they heard him ask someone to bring the drinks and water for the dog. Definitely not your average rancher, Violet thought again.

"Now if you don't mind, Mr. Clayton," said Hugh. "You said you wanted to talk to Violet—Mrs. Vaughn."

"If I'm not mistaken, it was you who were trespassing on my land. I think you should tell me what you're doing here and what you want. Please, have a seat," he gestured.

"That's fair," said Violet. She and Hugh sat side by side on the leather sofa and Red sat opposite them in an armchair.

"You had a dispute with Jim," said Violet, deciding to keep it simple.

Red steepled his hands in front of him, his face impassive. "That's no secret. But you want to know what the dispute was about. And was that enough to kill him?"

They were interrupted by a middle-aged Hispanic woman entering the room, carrying a tray, which she set on a square pine coffee table. Ice water sparkled in a crystal pitcher next to glasses and an assortment of cookies. Violet noticed slices of lemon and lime dancing in the ice water. Red Clayton was definitely living his best life.

"I put water for the dog outside," the woman said, pointing at the French doors.

"Thank you, Rosa," said Red. The woman exited the way she came. Entertaining guests here appeared to be a common occurrence.

The rancher returned his attention to Violet and Hugh.

"Jim Vaughn happened upon my father in a bar in Coatimundi many years ago. At that time, my dear old dad was on his way to drinking and gambling away my family legacy. On a bender and short on cash, he up and sold a piece of the ranch to Jim—for a pittance." His lips curled with bitterness.

"It didn't matter much for all those years. No one was living there, and it was like we still owned it. Luckily—and I mean that—dear old dad got drunk and wandered into the desert on a summer day. They didn't find him for a week. When they did, he was nothing but bones. Coyotes," he added, as if that explained everything.

Violet and Hugh looked at him with mixed expressions of horror and expectation.

"Suffice it to say, with a lot of hard work I brought the ranch back from disaster. It's almost back to its original glory. Almost." He leaned forward and took a cookie off the tray.

"I decided to make some uh—improvements— to the ranch. Improvements that require access to Jim's property. About that time, Jim showed up and set up camp. He hadn't been out here—ever. But all of a sudden, here he was. I made him a generous offer for the land. He refused. So I made him an even better offer, way more than the land is worth, I'll tell you that. You know what he said? He said he didn't need the money. Told me to piss off."

He hadn't taken a bite from the cookie, but used it to point at Violet and Hugh, emphasizing his points.

"I thought about what to do. And yes, murder might have even crossed my mind. But someone beat me to it. If it was you, my hat's off to you." At that, he took a crunching bite of his cookie.

"So if it wasn't you, who was it?" asked Hugh.

Red rubbed his chin. "I don't know, but I wouldn't be surprised if that trash he had living there had a part in it. Jennifer."

"Maven says Jennifer doesn't have the brains to pull something like that off," said Violet, taking a third cookie from the tray. Today wasn't the day to stop stress eating.

"I wouldn't be so sure. She's always been desperate to improve her standing—but she's not stupid."

"You said you wanted to talk to me," said Violet. "I expect you're going to make me an offer on the land that I can't refuse?"

"Exactly." Red, brightened. "I'm prepared to make you the same offer I made to your dear departed husband. What are you going to do with that land? You're a city girl, you don't want to stay in this dusty old place."

"The truth is, Mr. Clayton, it's not mine to sell

right now. All of Jim's assets have been frozen. Even if they find his missing cash, I expect it will be years for them to sort things out. Everything will probably get liquidated. I'll be lucky if I get the money that I'm out."

"I thought you might say that," said Red. "But I have a little ace in the hole, so to speak. A senator who owes me a favor. I think we could find a way around the little problem of the land, seeing as it's out here in New Mexico and Jim's crimes were in a different state. You could walk away with a nice little bit of cash, Mrs. Vaughn. Think about it."

"I will think about it," said Violet.

"When you say generous offer, just how generous are we talking about?" asked Hugh.

"I need the lawyers around to give you an exact number, but we're talking six figures. Not bad for a little piece of land Jim paid $500 for."

Over Red's shoulder, Violet noticed a photograph on the shelf. Red, his son and his daughter posed with a pretty woman with long dark hair.

"What about Mrs. Clayton?" she asked. "Shouldn't she be involved in this?"

Red looked startled. Or maybe, Violet thought, even frightened.

"No," he stammered, "my wife isn't involved in business matters. She's away right now—visiting relatives."

After an awkward silence, Violet stood up. "I'll think about your offer, Mr. Clayton. I'm sure you can appreciate that I have my hands full right now. But I'll let you know."

Hugh, Violet and Spirit walked back up the road to their truck.

"Did you get some creepy vibes when I mentioned his wife?" said Violet.

"Hell, that whole meeting was creepy. The story about his dad? Right out of a horror movie." Hugh stopped and placed a hand on Violet's arm. "Steer clear of him, alright? Don't meet that guy alone—he's not okay."

Violet nodded. "I think I'm safe from Red as long as he thinks I might sell him the land. But what's so important about that piece of property? There's something more to it. Nothing out here adds up."

Up ahead Spirit began barking his head off. Out of the brush, a trio of coatimundi ran across the road, their long strange tails in the air.

"Coatimundi," said Hugh, shaking his head.

Nothing more needed to be said.

CHAPTER 16

"You were right about the home sale documents being notarized," Violet told Hugh on the drive back to town. "Jim must have had a stand-in for me and fooled the notary."

"You need to give those documents to Montoya."

"I will. But there's one document I'm not going to give her quite yet. There's a copy of the deed to Jim's land. It's marked Sunset Title, that place we saw in Coatimundi. I want to go check it out. Plus, that deed might come into play if I need to sell the property."

Hugh nodded. "What do you say we take in some of the Mundi Madness festivities? While we're down there, we can look into the title place"

Spirit's head rested on her leg—he was out cold. "Okay, but I need to bring Spirit home, I think he needs some rest and quiet."

"Now you're thinking like a dog mom."

Violet opened the door of her RVand noticed it

wasn't completely latched. Looking back, she wasn't certain she had locked it. She must have, but lately she had so much on her mind, she didn't know which end was up.

Spirit bounced up into the RV and immediately put his nose to the floor, sniffing ferociously. This didn't worry her, seeing that the RV was previously a college party wagon. Who knows what kind of smells had become imbedded in the place. Ugh, she tried not to think about that. Spirit focused on the area where her high-heeled boots were. She had placed them there after donning her new boots. The key word being *were.* Because now an empty space of dark brown 1980's carpet glared back at her. She did a quick canvas of the place, which, in the small RV took about sixty seconds. Her boots were gone. Nothing else seemed to be missing, not that she had many possessions.

She emerged from the RV to find Hugh waiting for her.

"I've been robbed!" she said, stumbling down the steps.

Hugh reached to steady her. "What? What did they take?"

"My boots!"

"Is that all?"

"Is that *all*? Those are Balenciaga boots! Granted, they came into the thrift store as a donation, but they're valuable and they're mine. And just—why?"

"Let's get Maven and see if she saw anything,"

said Hugh, and he walked off toward the office.

Outside ,Violet sat down in a folding chair. Her stomach twisted in knots at the violation. Someone had been inside her home, such as it was. She clutched her large purse in her lap, grateful she had thought to put Jim's documents into it before leaving. She wondered momentarily if the boot thief might have been searching for them. But the boots and the documents didn't seem to have anything to do with each other.

In short order, Maven strode up the road, turquoise jangling, hippie skirt whirling in the breeze, looking uncharacteristically stern. Hugh and Maddie trailed behind.

"I don't tolerate thieves in my park," she said, as she approached Violet. "Now what's gone missing? Some boots?"

"Yes," said Violet, "I think that's it. I don't understand why someone would only take those."

"Perhaps it's a fetishist," Hugh said.

Violet raised an eyebrow. "I'm sorry?"

"You know, one of those blokes who fancies women's shoes."

"A pervert," Maven added.

Maddie rolled her eyes. "Alternative lifestyle."

"Did you see anyone hanging out here or headed this way?" asked Violet.

"No," said Maven, "And I've been in the office all day. I saw you folks leave in the truck earlier and of course Mundi Madness people have been coming and going, but no one—suspicious."

"I think we should call the sheriff," said Hugh. Maven and Maddie nodded in agreement.

"No!" Violet shouted, having a visceral reaction to the word sheriff. The other three blanched.

"No," she said again, more calmly. "I don't want any unnecessary interaction with the sheriff. I'll just let it go. I have these beautiful new boots to wear."

Maven and Maddie oohed and aahed, admiring her new boots. Violet stood up. "Let's just move on with our plans. I don't think there's much we can do."

She went back in the RV and put fresh food and water out for Spirit then patted the bed. "Come on buddy, you need some rest. I'll be back soon." The dog collapsed on the bed with a sigh. She knew she needed to get a dog bed and added that to her to-do list.

Her paycheck would hit her bank account tomorrow. Had that much time really gone by? The two weeks she took off work were flying past. To the growing list, she added call her boss. She honestly wasn't sure when—or if, she would return to her old life. Even if things resolved here in New Mexico, long buried thoughts and feelings were bubbling up to the surface. Some of those things she had tried to push down, tried to forget. But other things—more important things—were mixed in. Like finding out there were parts of herself, interests and skills, that she didn't know existed. She was more—capable of more—than she thought. It felt scary and wonderful at the same time.

She strolled down Main Street with Hugh. Booths, displays and entertainment decorated the blocked-off street. They got ice cream cones from a little cart and stopped to watch a group of fire eaters dressed in gothic black and red costumes. They were very close to Sunset Title, so after finishing their sweets, they headed inside the storefront office.

A buzzer sounded as they entered, the feeble noise more a wheeze than a buzz. The drab interior stood in stark contrast to the rest of Coatimundi. A single picture hung on the beige walls—a dusty generic painting of a snowy mountain scene. The back of the room housed rows of tan file cabinets. Two gray metal desks and a smattering of ugly office furniture filled the rest of the space. At one of the desks sat the only employee in the room, a woman so pale and plain Violet initially didn't notice her. With her gray-blonde hair and beige cardigan, she was essentially camouflaged. The woman watched them approach her desk with no question or animation in her eyes, just dull resignation.

"The bathrooms aren't for public use," she said robotically. "There's port-o-potties next to the bank."

"Oh—no, we need some information about a deed," said Violet.

The woman turned to her computer. "Name?"

"No, well, it's my husband's property. He must have come in here a while back to get the title, I just thought—"

"Name?" the woman repeated, hands hovering over the keyboard.

"His name is—was—Jim Vaughn."

The woman's hovering fingers froze on the

keyboard. She looked up at Hugh and Violet and really saw them for the first time. The blank eyes were now alight with interest as they flicked back and forth between them. Over the woman's shoulder, Violet saw a credenza crammed with pictures. They appeared to be all of one person, from baby to grown woman. And Violet knew that grown woman. Jennifer Norris.

"What do you want to know about the title?" she asked.

"I think you already know who I am," said Violet. "And I think I know who you are, too. Are you Mrs. Norris? Jennifer's mom?"

The woman remained frozen and Violet regretted her confrontational approach. Luckily, she had Hugh, who leaned forward to look at the pictures.

"Is *that* Jennifer?" he said. "What a beauty, you must be a proud mum."

At that, color flooded the woman as if painted with a brush. She smiled and rolled her chair back to gaze on the pictures herself.

"Yes. That's my Jennifer."

"Lovely, charming," said Hugh. "Now what's that one in the middle, was she homecoming queen?"

Mrs. Norris' face darkened again and she rolled back to her computer.

"Well her name isn't *Clayton*, so she wasn't homecoming queen. She was runner-up. Prettier than all of them. Anyone could see that. She was going to be a model, signed with an agency in Albuquerque. That would have shown them." Her eyes narrowed and she appeared lost in past grievances.

"She never became a model?" Hugh prodded gently.

"No, she blew it. Went and married the first loser that came her way, a *musician*. She wasted her youth on him and finally came home a few years ago. She works here with me now." She pointed at the other desk.

"This must be where she met Jim," Violet said.

Mrs. Norris looked startled.

"It's okay," Violet said, "I know that she and Jim were—close."

"Yes. Jim came in about a year ago. He wanted the deed for his land. He said he planned to move here. He was different than the men around town. He wore a suit and tie, he acted confident, he flashed money around. Jennifer really took to him. And I did, too. We didn't know he was married."

"I'm sure you were shocked by his death," said Hugh. Mrs. Norris nodded sadly.

Violet resigned herself to the bad cop role. "Jennifer lived with Jim when he was killed. Where was she the night he died?"

Mrs. Norris didn't appear to be bothered by the direct question, almost as if she were expecting it. "She was working late on the Mundi Madness floats—with Sheriff Winters. They've always had a —special relationship." Violet had to restrain herself from looking at Hugh and shouting out *What? Jennifer Norris and Sheriff Winters?* Instead she did her best to look impassive.

"My Jennifer couldn't hurt a soul," Mrs. Norris

continued. "Besides, it's pretty obvious who did it."

Here we go again, Violet thought. "And who is that?"

"Red Clayton." She gave a definitive nod of her head. "I'm not afraid to say what everyone else is thinking."

Violet sagged with relief to learn that she and Hugh were no longer the only suspects, at least in the eyes of the community.

"Clayton didn't get his way and he hates that. No one says no to a Clayton around here." Her eyes drifted to the homecoming picture.

"Of course, when Jim ended up dead, everyone said you did it, Mrs. Vaughn. You and your English friend. But when that private investigator turned up in the desert, shot in the back—well now, that says Clayton."

Violet and Hugh exchanged looks.

"He's just walking around, free as you please. Of course, his boy's a sheriff's deputy, what does that tell you?" She turned back to her computer screen. "You came in here for something, now what was it?"

"I think you've already answered my questions," said Violet. "Thank you for your time."

Violet and Hugh headed back down Main Street toward Maven's.

"The plot thickens," said Hugh. "Jan and her brothers can't be excluded as suspects. Red Clayton is also high on the list. And Jennifer's alibi is Sheriff Winters?"

Violet stopped mid-stride and grabbed Hugh's arm. "The sheriff is a suspect too." She spoke slowly as everything clicked into place. "He had a, what was it, *special relationship* with Jennifer. He could have killed Jim out of jealousy."

"And then killed the P.I. for what he knew?"

"He did have access to guns and could have tricked Denzer to get him out in the desert. But somehow...it seems like a stretch. He may be ornery, but he is a law enforcement officer, after all."

"But maybe not a stretch to think Sheriff Winters is protecting Jennifer," mused Hugh as they continued walking.

Violet stopped mid-stride and grabbed Hugh's arm. "I have to talk to Montoya right away. I need to let her know the sheriff may be compromised."

They headed back to their RVs, arm in arm, deep in discussion about the case. Hugh walked Violet to her door. She unlocked it and Spirit leapt out, tail wagging, then ran over to Hugh's lot. They laughed at his antics and followed the dog next door. Suddenly, Violet noticed someone sitting in a folding chair in front of Hugh's place. Seeing them, the woman stood up. Tall, slim and attractive, the brunette's hair was expertly coiffed in an elegant bun. From her expensive-looking white linen outfit to her designer handbag, she did not look like she belonged in an RV park in Coatimundi.

"Hugh, darling," she called. "Surprise!"

Hugh froze.

"Samantha." He practically spat the name out.

The woman glided forward, meeting Hugh and Violet where they stood. "After your last email, I felt I *had* to come and see if I could be of assistance. What's this about a murder? And you're a suspect? It's very unlike you to be so adventurous, Hugh." Her upper-crust British accent and manners could not be faulted in their perfection, and yet, Violet heard an edge to the woman's voice.

"You should have let me know you were coming," Hugh said quietly. "Your help isn't needed."

Samantha's eyes veered over to take in Violet. "Yes, it does look like you're—managing." She stretched her hand out to Violet. "Samantha Gordon—Hugh's wife."

Violet felt a rushing in her ears. She gave Samantha's hand a weak shake and mumbled "Violet Vaughn." She became suddenly and acutely aware of her disheveled appearance—it had been a long day.

"You said in your email you don't have a solicitor," Samantha pressed on. "That's completely daft, and you know it, Hugh. Our daughter begged me to come and sort things out."

"You told Bella about this?"

She ignored the question and addressed Violet. "I'm sure Hugh's told you I'm a solicitor."

He hadn't told her, but she remained silent —rendered speechless by the complicated feelings wrestling inside her.

"You're not licensed to practice in the U.S." said Hugh.

Spirit stood in front of Samantha, tail wagging,

begging to be acknowledged. "Get away, doggie, shoo!" she said, backing away from him. "My firm has a branch in New York, they're working on things for me. Are you going to make me stand out here in the dirt all evening? I don't want that dog to get my pants dirty. I was going to get a room, but that hippie woman told me everything's booked up, some moody festival or something, so I'm going to have to bunk with you."

"I think I'd better—go," said Violet, backing away, wanting to extricate herself as quickly as possible. "Come on, Spirit."

"Wait—Violet—" Hugh said, but she had already turned to go. Not very far though. She found herself facing Sheriff Winters and Deputy Clayton striding toward her.

"Violet Vaughn," the Sheriff said, approaching her. "I'm placing you under arrest."

"What!" Violet and Hugh cried at the same time.

"For breaking and entering. Someone broke into the crime scene earlier today—Jim Vaughn's trailer. Left a bunch of footprints that look suspiciously like high-heeled boots—these to be precise." He pointed at Deputy Clayton who held up what appeared to be Violet's boots, in a plastic bag. "These were found in a garbage can right here in Maven's Haven. Everyone around town has seen you strutting around in those boots."

"But...but they were stolen!" Violet cried. "This morning!"

"Right," said the sheriff flatly. "I didn't get any reports of a break-in. Did you, Deputy Clayton?"

"No sir," he said, with a smirk.

"Let's go, Deep Dish," Sheriff Winters said, grabbing her arm. "You're going to jail."

CHAPTER 17

Violet walked down the long hallway of her old house in Chicago in total darkness. Why was it so dark? She couldn't find the light switch, it wasn't where it was supposed to be. She fumbled along, heading toward the master bedroom. She felt the striped wallpaper, could feel the raised pattern. At the door of the bedroom, her fingers reached for the switch. Blinding light filled the room. But it wasn't a room, it was a sandy desert. Jim's body lay on the ground, a knife buried in his chest. A vulture perched on his head, screeching.

She awoke with a gasp. Something solid pressed against her cheek. In front of her, she saw iron bars, and, further ahead an open door. Through the door she could see the back of Deputy Jones, sitting with his feet up on the desk, looking at his phone.

She sat up and felt her face where a deep groove had formed from laying on the hard wooden bench of the holding cell. More benches lined the sides of the bare bones enclosure. Violet's eyes landed on the stainless steel toilet, right out where anyone could see.

The sight brought tears to her eyes.

So this is it, she thought. After everything, this is how it's going to end up. She wasn't one to feel sorry for herself, but—she did. Just about as sorry as she could possibly be. Incarcerated. Alone. No family. No friends. And—she felt a pang in her heart—no Hugh. He and Samantha were probably having a nice dinner together right about now. Maybe they were even working things out—which was none of her business, she told herself. But still—she had come to think of herself and Hugh as a team. So much for their amateur investigation. Sheriff Winters had won. She was going to live out her days in a cell like this, for a crime she didn't commit—framed by some as yet unknown person in Coatimundi who killed Jim and the P.I., and, bewilderingly, stole her boots.

Sheriff Winters walked through the door and interrupted her pity party. Violet stood and approached the bars. "You can't keep me in here," she said. "Don't I get bail? Or to talk to a judge? I want to see Special Agent Montoya. I'll bet she doesn't know about this."

"You're all full of ideas, aren't you? Burglarizing a crime scene is a serious offense. So is destroying evidence."

"Destroying evidence? I have no idea what you're talking about."

The sheriff leaned casually against the wall opposite her. "That's what you were doing out there, right? Trying to cover your tracks?"

"I don't need to cover my tracks, because I didn't

kill Jim. If anyone needs to cover their tracks, it's you
—and your special friend, Jennifer."

Surprise showed on the sheriff's face, which
then contorted into anger and Violet felt good to be
able to deal him a blow. He leaned close to the bars.
"You think you know something, Deep Dish?" His
voice was low and threatening. "Well you don't know
skunk butt about me or this town. Let me tell you—"

"Sheriff?" Deputy Jones poked his head around
the door. "Someone's here—" He trailed off, looking
over his shoulder uncertainly.

The sheriff gave a final glare in Violet's direction
and exited. Through the door, she could see a small
slice of the outer room. Deputy Jones and Sheriff
Winters obscured the person, but Violet could hear a
woman's confident British accent, voice raised.

"Constable, my firm in New York is representing
Mrs. Vaughn and Dr. Gordon. You can't keep our client
here for one more minute." She banged on the front
desk in rhythm to the last three words. "We have
exonerating witnesses to account for Mrs. Vaughn's
whereabouts—and her footwear—for the entire day."

The door opened and Violet caught a glimpse
of Maven and Maddie coming in. Maven stood next to
Samantha and shook her head sadly. "I'm surprised at
you, Dan," she said to the sheriff.

The door opened again and Dr. Wauneka came
in, followed by his sister Grace, Special Agent Montoya
and finally—Hugh." Violet saw the tension on his face.
He hadn't been having a nice dinner with Samantha
after all. They were all here—for her.

Violet sat in one of Hugh's folding chairs in front of his fire pit, eating cheese and salami from a hastily-arranged snack tray. Everyone had come back to the RV park to compare stories of the evening's events. Maven, Maddie, Hugh, Samantha and Grace all joined Violet at the fire. In the distance, Montoya conversed with Dr. Wauneka. Violet had invited the agent to join them, but she declined and Violet understood. She saw Montoya lean in close to the doctor, listening intently. Violet hoped the vet was sharing the story about his sister.

After Violet's arrest, Hugh and Samantha had contacted witnesses to prove that she couldn't possibly have trespassed at Jim's place. Unable to get hold of the Waunekas, Hugh had driven all the way to White Feather to find them. They even spoke to Red Clayton, who called the sheriff to verify the timeframe of Hugh and Violet's visit with him. All of this had left Sheriff Winters hopping mad, but faced with the evidence, unable to continue to hold Violet.

She was begrudgingly grateful for Samantha's assistance. "Thank you for helping to get me out of there," she said, looking at Samantha. Then she smiled at the entire group. "Thank you, all of you, for showing up for me."

Samantha looked bored and brushed non-existent bugs from her high-end active wear. "Well, I can be useful at times." She sent a meaningful look toward Hugh. "I don't see any reason why you can't leave tomorrow. They have no evidence against you and can't legally keep you here."

Maven sat forward. "Leave? You can't! Tomorrow is the Mundi Moon Dance!"

Dr. Wauneka, now with the group, joined the others in a chorus of "Yes! Stay!"

Violet glanced at Hugh. "I am going to stay, at least for a few more days. I have more questions I need to ask to get to the bottom of Jim's death. I need to see this through."

"I'm not going to abandon ship now," said Hugh.

Samantha rolled her eyes and stood. "This has all been too much fun. I'm going to bed. Hugh, dear, can you help me get settled?"

Violet watched Hugh trail Samantha into the RV. She couldn't imagine what brought the two of them together in the first place. A pang of jealousy hit her gut. She tried again to push it down. She felt a hand on her arm—it was Maddie.

"It's going to work out," she said, watching Hugh as well. "They have unfinished business, but anyone can see the chemistry between you."

"It's none of my concern," said Violet turning back to the fire.

"It's your heart's concern," said Maddie, smiling. "And the heart does what the heart does."

Violet patted Spirit's head as he leaned against her leg. "Right now, my heart is happy to have friends." She looked around at the little group, talking and laughing around the fire. It was true. Getting arrested and put in jail was worth it to find out she had people in her life who cared about her. Well, almost worth it. She wouldn't want to stay behind bars any longer than she already had.

Her eyes landed on Dr. Wauneka, who had a far-off look as he stared into the fire. Violet could see pain and worry etched into the lines of both his and his sister's faces, a set to the upper brow that revealed the weight of their emotional journey.

Violet leaned in closer to the fire and addressed the doctor. "Is Agent Montoya going to help with your sister's case?"

Everyone turned toward him and Maven placed a hand on his arm. "Dearest Kai, I'd forgotten what you must be going through. I guess it must have been about a year now," she said, with concern.

The doctor forced a smile and sat up straighter. "Agent Montoya promised to look into it. She didn't know much about all the women killed in White Feather."

"I'm not surprised," said Grace. "Ninety-five percent of the cases of missing or murdered indigenous women aren't covered by the media. There's no way for anyone to know about Rainy or the others."

Violet sat up straighter, startled by the statistics. "Doctor, couldn't the Navajo Nation police investigate?"

"Please, call me Kai," he said with a smile. "Unfortunately, the Navajo police are stretched pretty thin. There's less than two hundred officers for 27,000 square miles."

"And also, there's jurisdictional issues," added Grace. "The Navajo Nation is like a separate country. But still, Rainy's car was found on the highway near Coatimundi. It seems like the sheriff could do more." Grace's shoulders slumped and she clasped her hands tightly in her lap. "The sheriff, he made it seem like it was Rainy's fault, that she shouldn't have been working late at a bar. But she'd made that trip hundreds of times..." Grace's voice trailed off,

Violet's eyes narrowed and she shook her head. Sheriff Winters. Ugh. An owl began to hoo-hoo-hoo startlingly close by. She had never heard an owl in real life. It was a lonely sound. I feel ya buddy, she thought.

"Have they found any evidence or clues as to what happened?" asked Maven.

Kai nodded. "The two women who disappeared from White Feather—Mirage Yazzi and Helena Begay —were both seen at separate times talking to a man in a white pickup truck. No one recognized him and no one really got a good look at him. They just described a white guy wearing a hoodie. And there was a witness who said they saw Rainy's car on the side of the road with a white pickup truck pulled up next to it." He shook his head sadly. "That's about all we've got."

Violet stood up and went to Grace, leaning over and giving her a hug. "I'm so sorry I brought this up. I've made you both sad."

Kai shook his head. "No, I'm glad you did. The day you and Hugh walked into my clinic, I had all but given up hope that we would ever find Rainy's killer. But you've breathed new life into the investigation.

Now, with Montoya's help, and Hugh's research, we might get somewhere."

After everyone left, Violet went to look for the owl, hoping to catch a glimpse of the creature in the darkness. His mournful sound seemed to be coming from somewhere between her and Hugh's rigs. She moved a little way, then stopped to listen. But just when she thought she was close to the owl, the farther away it sounded.

She looked back at Hugh's RV, where soft, warm light shone from the kitchen window. Stop it, she told herself and turned toward her own place. The pity party is over. She would find out who killed Jim so she could get some resolution. If the money turned up, that would be a nice bonus. There was one important person she hadn't talked to yet, and she would do that first thing tomorrow.

Spirit waited at her side, quiet and patient, his head tilted up, gazing at something in the distance. Violet followed his sightline to a tall and bulky saguaro cactus. Two orange orbs glowed. "Ohhh..." said Violet, moving closer to the glowing eyes. Suddenly, the cactus seemed to come alive as the enormous owl took flight, swooping toward her. She caught a glimpse of a round face framed by long, horn-like tufts. She ducked, covering her head —his talons looked huge and sharp. The owl gave an annoyed screech and Violet and Spirit were left staring into a black sky, speechless with wonder.

CHAPTER 18

"Great Horned Owl," Violet said to Spirit. He looked at her, head cocked, and then went back to smelling around in the brush near her RV. She sat in a folding chair, her new bird book in her lap. She had gotten up early so she could brew coffee, get dressed, and be outside in time to see the sun rise. It was worth it. The puffy cumulous clouds were alight with oranges and reds the color of fire embers. The chirping and singing of morning birds accelerated as the sky turned fuchsia, pink and finally a cool pale blue.

She arose this early for another reason. She sipped her coffee and looked out past the RV park where she could see the motel. Finally, the moment she was waiting for. One of the motel doors opened and an auburn-haired woman in a pink track suit emerged, her little dog pulling on the leash.

"Time to go," Violet said to Spirit, clipping on his lead. "Want to go for a walk?"
He answered in a flurry of spins, tail-wagging and jumps.

Violet assumed Jennifer would walk her dog

around the motel grounds as she had previously. The plan was to surreptitiously bump into Jennifer in order to question her. But Violet was surprised to see the woman head out to the main street, walking at a fast clip, as if she needed to be somewhere. Violet set off, but there was a good deal of distance to cover and Jennifer moved quickly.

By the time Violet reached the road, she could still see the pink tracksuit farther up the street. Jennifer's auburn ponytail bounced and swayed to the rhythm of her purposeful stride. Violet had to practically run to keep from losing her, which was fine with Spirit, who pulled on his lead, tongue lolling and eyes bright. As Jennifer reached the main part of town, she turned onto a side street. When Violet reached the same spot, she made a left as Jennifer had. She found herself staring at a chain link fence. A dead end. It was like she disappeared into thin air. Spirit kept pulling on his leash to move forward—he seemed to know something Violet didn't.

Closer inspection revealed a long alley bounded on one side by the back of the Main Street businesses. A chain link fence ran the length of the other side. Violet was just in time to see Jennifer stop at the far end of the corridor and pound on a metal roll-up door.

The garbage cans lining the alley overflowed with Mundi Madness refuse. Violet slipped around the corner and dashed for cover behind a group of green bins. She heard the opening of the rolling door. With another peek, she saw Jennifer greet someone, still standing outside the door.

"I need to see who she's talking to," Violet whispered to Spirit. He wagged his tail and continued to sniff the smelly garbage cans. Jennifer's back was slightly turned to her, so Violet made a move, running from one group of trash cans to the next. It was all a fun game to Spirit and he came along enthusiastically, smelling as he went. Finally, they made it to a group of cans fairly close to the rolling door and Violet strained to hear the conversation.

"So who found the gun?" Jennifer said.

"Montoya and her team. They're testing it now, but I'll bet it's the weapon that killed Denzer."

Sheriff Winters. Violet prayed she would not be seen. She took a quick look and saw Jennifer standing outside the roll-up door. The sheriff, situated slightly inside, was hidden from view. Violet could see crepe paper and tissue in the overflowing garbage can and determined this must be where the parade floats were built.

"Everything's just so weird right now," Jennifer said. "And Agent Montoya came to see me last night. It's really freaking me out."

"What did she want?"

"She wanted to know about our relationship, you know, me and you. That woman, Violet Vaughn, went and blabbed to her."

"Violet Vaughn." He spit the name out with such derision he need not say anymore on the subject. The feeling's mutual, Violet thought.

"So what did you tell her?" the sheriff stepped

out of the garage and into the alley. Spirit began to strain at his leash. Violet peered between the cans and saw Jennifer's Chihuahua also pulling on her lead, eyes fixed on Violet's hiding place.

"I told her the truth. That we're just friends," said Jennifer.

The sheriff ran his hands through his hair and shook his head. "No. *You're* just friends Jennifer. That's your own point of view."

"What does that mean?"

"You don't know what it means? After all this time?"

Oh brother, Violet thought. As much as she disliked the sheriff, she felt awkward eavesdropping on what was potentially going to be a love declaration. And now that he had stepped into the alley, there was no way for Violet to retrace her steps without being seen.

"Why didn't you say something before?" asked Jennifer.

"I didn't really have much of a window, did I? After your marriage to that drummer you came back to town and then hooked up with that—that slime bag from Chicago."

Aha, thought Violet. The sheriff's hatred of Chicago—and herself personally—had nothing to do with the city itself. It was the oldest reason in the book —heartbreak.

Jennifer stepped closer to Sheriff Winters. "The last time I saw Jim, he had just told me he was married and he would never divorce his wife. That's why I came to find you that night. I just wanted to be with you. Luckily, we worked on floats that whole evening, or you might have thought I killed him. And that's when I realized—"

Whatever Jennifer realized was drowned out by a sudden explosive grinding sound from the end of the alley behind Violet. A monstrous green garbage truck appeared, barely squeezing into the narrow channel. It screeched, puffed and steamed as it maneuvered to pick up the first row of cans. It was going to arrive at Violet's hiding place shortly. She peeked again at the couple, now clasped together in an embrace. Princess barked in the direction where she and Spirit hid as the garbage truck churned down the passageway.

Violet started to sweat, panic filling her. Spirit had become agitated, pacing and spinning and managed to get his leash wrapped around her ankles. She tried to move and ending up falling over onto her side in a fetal position, the leash hopelessly tangling her feet. The garbage truck grinded forward, puffing as it stopped at the next set of cans. She pulled and wrestled with the leash, finally freeing her feet.

Jennifer and Sheriff Winters were now in a full-blown make-out session. Spirit, still agitated by the garbage truck, pulled tight on the leash. Violet lost her grasp and he bolted across the alley. She heard the garbage truck moving again, and saw it was nearly on top of her.

And then—miraculously, she saw her dog on the other side of the chain link fence, looking back at her and waiting. There must be a gap in the fence, she thought. Heart pounding, she took one more glance at the kissing couple and darted across the alley. She saw the gap and shimmied through, just as the garbage truck reached her hiding place. She followed Spirit as he bounded across an empty lot.

Stumbling over sagebrush and rocks, Violet finally reached her dog. He sat at the edge of a road, calmly waiting for her. She knelt down and hugged him tight. "You are a good, good boy, good dog," she said into his fur. "Now let's get out of here."

Ten minutes later, Violet sat at an outdoor table at Coati Coffee, sipping a chamomile tea while Spirit drank water from a cup. She tried to mentally unpack everything she had just learned from her spy mission as she waited for the tea to calm her nerves.

Sheriff Winters and Jennifer indeed had a special relationship. But they obviously had an alibi for the night Jim was killed— they were working on parade floats. More importantly, she learned that a potential murder weapon had been found. Whose gun was it and who killed Jim and Denzer? She felt no closer to an answer than in the beginning of this mess.

She found an ATM and withdrew some much-needed cash. On the way back to Maven's, she looked through some of the festival booths. At a place selling Native American goods, she found a cozy-looking dog bed for Spirit, and a hand-woven collar. A dress caught her eye—gauzy white cotton and ankle-length. She did need something to wear to the Mundi Moon Dance, she thought, and decided to splurge.

Violet arrived at Maven's Haven just in time to see Jan and her brothers pile into a cab and drive away. She stopped in the office to get the scoop from the innkeeper.

"They're outta here," Maven said with a wink. "The word is, the FBI is calling off the search for the money. No reason for those folks to stick around—unless of course they're the killers. But come to think of it, if they were the killers, they probably would have left a long time ago."

Violet, leaned on the counter. "I think you're right. I don't think they did it."

"Have you found any new information, Miss Detective?"

"Did you know Jennifer Norris and Sheriff Winters are—a thing?"

Maven slapped the counter and laughed. Then she yelled into the back office, "Hey Maddie, Violet wants to know if Jennifer and Dan have something goin' on!"

Violet heard a laugh from the back.

"Of course we know," Maven continued. "The whole town knows. Dan's been mooning after Jennifer since they were in high school. Of course, Jen's mama had bigger plans for her, so I think she discouraged it. But he ain't lookin' so bad now, especially after that disaster marriage and then Jim."

"Trust me, anyone's better than Jim. Even Sheriff Winters. But one thing's clear. It would take an ace detective to find out any new information in this town. Everybody knows everything."

"It seems that way, don't it?" Maven leaned in close over the counter. "Don't be fooled though. This town's got a mess of secrets—stuff that's just simmering under the surface, and you never know when it's gonna boil over."

"I haven't figured out much more about my own mystery. The more I look, the less I know. Right now I'll settle for them not arresting me or Hugh."

"Come on down to the Moon Dance tonight, that will get your mind off things. Starts with the Moon Parade at sundown."

"Hey, speaking of the dance, do you have some kind of Southwestern belt I can borrow for tonight?"

Maven left and returned shortly with exactly what Violet was looking for.

She really wanted to talk to Hugh, but when she stopped by his RV he and Samantha sat close together outside, deep in discussion. "I guess it's just you and me," she said to Spirit, and she climbed into her own RV with a heavy heart.

CHAPTER 19

Violet stepped back to take a final look in the mirror. Not too bad, she thought. She wore the new white dress and her Navajo boots. She finished the look with the brown leather belt from Maven, heavily embellished with silver and turquoise. Maven told her it was called a Concho belt, made by traditional Navajo artisans.

She gave a quick pat to Spirit who rested comfortably in his new dog bed and then left, making sure to lock her door. She headed in the direction of Hugh's place. She had given him some space, but now she wanted to talk to her friend. And she definitely didn't want to head off to the festivities by herself.

She knocked on the door. Nothing. She knocked again. Still no answer. Disappointed, she trudged off down the gravel path. Once or twice, she looked back over her shoulder, just in case he came to the door, but his place remained silent and still.

She could see other people walking in the direction of the road, so she followed them into town. As she walked, she thought about the idea of a life change. Leaving Chicago and now being constantly confronted with thoughts of Jim had made one thing clear. She had never fully dealt with the scars from domestic violence.

She had carefully constructed a life that was safe. But maybe too safe. She hadn't let anyone in, not even friends. Being forced out of that comfort zone made her realize in a very short time everything she had been missing.

But staying in Coatimundi was a crazy idea. She should just head back to Chicago, keep her job and think about making some changes there. Maybe start some counseling. As long as the sheriff actually let her leave town, she thought wryly.

People lined the sides of the street, getting ready for the event. A parade at sundown seemed like a strange idea. Weren't they mostly in the daytime? Just another weirdness of Crazymundi, as Hugh called it.

Oh Hugh, she thought, why have you abandoned me? No, that's not fair, he's not responsible for entertaining me, she argued with herself. One thing was for sure—this place wasn't the same without him. Why am I feeling sorry for myself again, she thought, what is wrong with me?

She found a place to stand along the road. It was beginning to get dark and she noticed the street lights were not lit. Music started and a hush fell over the gathering. Up the street, she saw a glow and then, out of the darkness, emerged the first float. Covered with tiny sparkling lights, it glittered magically in the near dark. As it came closer, she saw it was an enormous coatimundi, surrounded by blooming cacti. The crowd applauded and cheered.

Something compelled Violet to look over her shoulder. There, jogging up the street, was Hugh. He scanned the crowd, his eyes searching. She threw her arm in the air and waved wildly. Finally, he saw her and hurried over. This was the first time she had ever seen him not wearing a sweater vest. He wore jeans, a white button-down shirt and a navy blazer. When he reached Violet, he pulled her into a hug.

"I've been looking everywhere for you," he said in her ear. "You left without me."

"I knocked at your door. I thought you might be —busy with Samantha." She didn't let go of the hug.

"No, I must have been in the shower. Samantha's gone."

Violet pulled away. "Gone? Where?"

"Home. Come on, let's watch the parade, I'll tell you about it later. You look beautiful, by the way." He took her hand and they stood side by side. The negative thoughts weighing Violet down evaporated and she watched the parade with new eyes. The lighted floats showcased Southwestern art and culture, each one more exquisite than the next.

One of the floats featured a pretty girl with a sash and crown, her pink dress covered entirely with twinkle lights.

"It's Red Clayton's daughter, Bailey," Violet said.

"I guess the reign of the Claytons continues," Hugh said, leaning close to her ear so she could hear him over the crowd sounds.

Another float represented the Navajo Nation, with young people dressed in traditional clothing, everything alight in vibrant colors. Violet recognized Dr. Wauneka's vet tech, looking gorgeous in a flowing red dress.

When the parade ended, everyone started moving up the street. A friendly, merry feeling hung in the air, the sound of animated voices and laughter carrying into the night. Violet and Hugh allowed themselves to be drawn along with the crowd.

"I can see why Sheriff Winters takes his float duties so seriously," said Hugh. "That was the most beautiful parade I've ever seen."

"It was magical," agreed Violet. "I think the sheriff might have been inspired—by love."

"Oh really? Do tell."

They walked arm in arm and Violet relayed the story of the day's events, what she'd witnessed and heard.

"Spirit saved me. If it wasn't for him, I would have been forced out of my hiding place and the sheriff would have seen me."

"I'm sorry I wasn't there with you," said Hugh, giving her arm a squeeze.

At the far end of town, the crowd filtered out into an empty lot. A raised dance floor had been constructed and a band played lively country music from the stage. Some couples were already out on the floor, dancing.

"Look, it's Kai and Grace," said Violet. The doctor noticed them and waved them over.

"Hello, are you enjoying the evening?" asked Violet.

"Yes," said Kai, giving them a warm smile, "But I was hoping to see Rosie here, have you seen her?"

Violet and Hugh looked at him blankly. "Who's Rosie?" asked Hugh.

"Agent Montoya," said Kai. "I, um—had some questions for her."

Was he blushing, Violet wondered. If he was, she wished him luck with the hard-nosed agent. She doubted Montoya was the type to let her hair down and mingle with the locals.

While Hugh chatted with Kai, Violet took in the crowd. She saw Maven and Maddie chatting and laughing with a group. On the other side of the dance floor, the Clayton clan gathered. Red Clayton, dressed in upscale western-wear, talked to a group of similarly-clad men. Bailey Clayton, now changed out of her parade dress, still wore her crown and was surrounded by a group of girlfriends. Brody Clayton, the sheriff's deputy, wore street clothes and leaned in close to a pretty blond girl.

In another corner, Jennifer Norris stood drinking some punch, her mother next to her. Jennifer looked radiant in an emerald green dress, her auburn hair floating around her shoulders. Her mother still wore her beige cardigan, a contrast that might have been intentional, Violet mused, so as to make Jennifer shine even brighter. A thought struck Violet and she looked back and forth between Jennifer and Red Clayton. There was a striking similarity between them. They could practically be brother and sister. She realized Hugh was speaking to her.

"You're lost in thought," he said. "I was asking if you wanted to dance."

Violet realized the band had begun to play a slow country tune. Some couples left the dance floor, while others grabbed their partners by the hand and pulled them out to share a romantic slow dance.

Violet allowed Hugh to guide her to the floor. They began to sway in time to the music and she put her head on Hugh's shoulder, her mind still tingling with an idea she couldn't quite put together. Then Hugh was talking to her again.

"The main reason Samantha came here was to go over our divorce papers. We had some things to iron out, but we were able to do it amicably. I signed the papers."

"So...that's it?" Violet said. "You're divorced?"

"We have to wait for the papers to be filed, but yes, it's happening." He tightened his grasp on her waist.

"That's...that's good," said Violet. "If that's what you want, then I'm glad for you. I mean, I'm sorry about your marriage, but—"

They were interrupted by a commotion. Many of the couples stopped dancing and gaped at something going on nearby. Hugh and Violet tried to get a look.

Sheriff Winters, Special Agent Montoya and a few other officers waded through the crowd, with purpose. Everyone parted to let them get by as they walked all the way around the dance floor. Violet's heart jumped to her throat, sure that this was it—they were coming to get her after all. She clung to Hugh and he pulled her close. But the officers did not even glance her way. They continued on and stopped in front of the Clayton family.

Sheriff Winters stepped to the front. "Red Clayton. You're under arrest for the murders of Jim Vaughn and C.J. Denzer."

The band stopped playing and silence fell as the good cheer was sucked right out of the crowd.

Red held his head high and stared the sheriff down. "There must be some mistake, Winters. I didn't kill anybody. What kind of stupid prank is this?"

"We can trace both of the murder weapons to you, Clayton," said the sheriff. "We got you."

"What?" said Red, incredulous. "The murder weapons? That's impossible. I—I didn't do it!"

"Let's go, Mr. Clayton," said Montoya. "You'll get the chance to tell your side."

Brody Clayton pushed forward. "No, sheriff! Don't do this! You've got it wrong, my dad would never —"

Sheriff Winters put his hand up. "Sorry, son. The evidence speaks for itself. Go take care of your family."

With that, they led Red Clayton away. Everyone could hear him shouting, proclaiming his innocence. In an instant, a cacophony of chatter started up, everyone undoubtedly gossiping about the shocking events. The band began to play and Hugh brought

Violet in close to continue their dance.

"I really didn't see that coming," said Hugh. "I'm usually a good judge of character. When we talked to him, I didn't get the feeling he was involved. Well, maybe involved in some other nefarious stuff, but not this."

"Yes," said Violet. "Something's—not right. I can't put my finger on it, but I think they might have the wrong man."

In the distance, she could see Red being placed in a police car. Her gaze fell on Jennifer Norris' mom. The woman stood with arms crossed, lips pursed, her head nodding ever so slightly as her eyes followed Red Clayton. For some reason, Jim's letter came to Violet's mind and his words. *Vultures are everywhere.*

CHAPTER 20

"It all seems so neat and tidy." Violet's hand rested on Spirit as she looked over at Hugh. "I swear, I didn't get the feeling Red killed Jim." She found herself again in the beat up truck with Hugh, travelling toward the Navajo Nation.

"He did have means, motive and opportunity," said Hugh, one hand on the steering wheel, the other resting casually on the back of the seat. "With Jim out of the way, he could approach you about buying the land."

"True. But he doesn't strike me as the type to get his hands dirty. I keep thinking about Jennifer or Sheriff Winters...and...and...Jennifer's mom sure does hate the Clayton family, although I don't know why she would kill Jim and Denzer. Or maybe we should have looked closer at Jan and her brothers?"

Hugh was chuckling and shaking his head. "I think you were enjoying the detective work and don't want to let it go. Usually, the simplest explanation is the best. Winters and Jennifer have an alibi. Jan and family came to get their mom's money, not kill someone. I do think Mrs. Norris is tickled pink to see the Claytons go down, but she doesn't look like she has it in her to stab a man and then shoot another with a shot gun."

Violet shrugged her shoulders. "Yeah. I guess."

"Maybe I snuck out and did it, did you ever think of that?" Hugh turned toward her and contorted his face, waggling his eyebrows. "Hugh the Ripper."

Violet laughed. "I think we've already established you're a serial helper, not serial killer."

"Just relax and enjoy not being a suspect anymore. They've got somebody, we're off the hook, and we can move on." He glanced over and gave her a little smile. "Thank you for coming with me today."

"You think seeing where they found Rainy Wauneka's body will help in your research?"

"Kai was already going to be out there today with Montoya. He thought I might want to see it. Actually, that leads me to something else I wanted to talk to you about. I've decided I'm going to write a book about the missing women from White Feather. Kai's already given me enough information to see that we're probably dealing with a serial killer. I think a book could bring awareness—and maybe even help solve it."

"That's—that's wonderful, I know you'll do a good job. But I think there's more, right?"

"Right. I'm going to stay in Coatimundi while I work on the book, which could be for some time. And I was wondering—I was hoping—you might stay too."

Spirit, sitting between them, followed the

conversation, his head moving from one to the other as they spoke. Violet gave a little smile to Hugh and then looked out the window at the sandstone zooming by, sage and cacti sprouting out from between the cracks in the rock.

She let out a sigh. "The truth is, I don't know what I'm going to do. My nest egg was stolen by Jim. Who knows if I'll ever see any of that money. And it looks like Red's offer of buying the land is off the table. I'm not a person of means. I have to make good decisions for myself—I can't just follow my heart."

Hugh pulled in a breath like he was going to speak, but then Violet pointed. "Look—isn't that the turnoff we're supposed to take?"

Hugh turned onto a narrow sandy road. They saw Dr. Wauneka's veterinary truck parked at the side as well as the generic government-issue car belonging to Montoya. As they exited the truck, they spied Kai and Montoya making their way back toward the vehicles. Montoya wore khaki pants, black hiking boots and a black T shirt, her hair in its neat bun. Kai looked handsome as usual in jeans and a western shirt. When Montoya spotted Hugh and Violet, she shook her head back and forth and then looked toward the sky in what might have been a prayer for patience. Kai, on the other hand, gave them a big wave.

Montoya strode toward them. "What are you two doing out here?" Direct, as usual. "You're in the clear. Shouldn't you be headed out to Florida or something?"

"Why are you still here?" asked Hugh. "Don't you need to go back to Chicago eventually?"

"I, unlike you, have an official reason to be here, Dr. Gordon. I've asked to be assigned to the White Feather murders. I'm here conducting an investigation. So, I repeat, what are you two doing here?"

Kai stepped forward. "Actually, I invited Dr. Gordon in a professional capacity. He's writing a book about the murders."

"Just perfect," said Montoya, shaking her head. She exhaled a long breath. "I'm sure you're going to clear everything—and I mean everything—with me before you go questioning anyone."

"Sure thing," said Hugh, giving an exaggerated wink. "So, Kai—what can you show me out here?"

"There's a stone marker about a hundred yards in that direction." He turned and pointed in the area he and Montoya came from. "That's—that's where they found her." His voice cracked and his lips began to tremble.

Violet reached out and patted his shoulder. Spirit bounded up and nuzzled his hand.

"It's the Spirit dog," he said. He knelt down to pet the dog and ran his hands expertly over the animal in a quick examination. "He looks good."

Montoya, never able to resist the dog, knelt next to Kai. She and the vet shared a quiet moment side by side, petting Spirit. It came to Violet's mind that he would be a good therapy dog—he had a calming effect on people.

Montoya finally stood up and put her hands on her hips. "We're going to get this guy. We'll get justice for your sister and the other women. I'll be in touch, doctor."

When she saw both Hugh and Kai nod at her, she clarified. "Dr. *Wauneka*." Then she strode toward her car.

After Montoya left, Violet let Kai know she was planning a dinner party that evening back at Maven's Haven. "Be sure to invite Grace as well," she called after the vet as he walked toward his truck. He gave a little wave in acknowledgement.

"I want to go find that marker," said Hugh. "I just want to look around for a few minutes."

They picked their way over rocks, brush and thistles. A sweep of wind kicked up a dust devil, whipping Violet's hair and pelting her cheeks with tiny specks of debris. A pile of smooth, white sand stones signaled they had found the spot.

"It's pretty desolate," said Violet, turning in a circle as she surveyed the view.

"Yes. But still, it's close enough to the highway that it could be an out-of-towner or a local. My gut tells me local, or at least someone who passes through frequently, seeing as there are multiple victims in this area."

Hugh began poking into some of the brush close to the marker.

"What are you looking for?" asked Violet.

"Just any little thing. Anything unusual or out of place. It was a year ago, so it's doubtful we'll find evidence. But from everything Kai says, they didn't do much of an investigation, so who knows."

Violet picked up a stick from the ground and used it to overturn rocks and peer into the scrubby undergrowth, her senses on alert for snakes. She found nothing man-made, not even an old soda can. Spirit sniffed under a thorny bush and Violet peered down and inside the shrub. Toward the bottom, she noticed something caught in the thorns. She used the stick to dislodge a pinkish-white piece of cardboard. She pulled it out and recognition hit her.

"Hey, look!"

Hugh came over and examined the object, a red-and-white checked serving tray. "We've seen this before. It's pretty faded, but there's no mistaking it."

"Yes, from the place with the Hatch chili peppers," said Violet.

"That's interesting. It's just a little ways up the highway from what I remember. Could be something, who knows."

They spent a few more minutes looking around, then made their way back to the truck.

"I want to get some of those chilies for my dinner tonight," said Violet.

"Good," said Hugh, "I can ask a few questions."

The chili vendor was the same man they had seen there before.

"Hey, Obi Wan," he said as they approached. "The force guided you back to my peppers."

Hugh laughed and did a mock light saber in

the air. "We did come for some chilies. But I was also hoping to ask you some questions."

The man crossed his arms and narrowed his eyes. "What kind of questions?"

Hugh pulled out the plastic bag with the faded cardboard tray. "Are there other businesses around here that use this kind of serving tray?"

The man's jaw set. "What's this about?"

Violet stepped forward. It's about the murder of Rainy Wauneka."

His eyes grew wide. "Rainy?"

"You knew her?" asked Hugh.

"Everybody knew Rainy. She was—she was special. We grew up together. So, how are you involved?"

"I'm researching the murders of the women in White Feather. I'm a forensic psychologist, writing a book about it. Kai Wauneka asked for my help. I'm Hugh, by the way, and this is Violet."

"I'm Kyle Dodge. But everyone calls me Dr. Pepper or Pep. Look, if you want answers around here, you're gonna have to work on your technique. People in these parts don't like questions from outsiders. But I'll help. For Rainy's sake, and Kai and Grace."

"So, the cardboard tray...?" Hugh prodded.

"Oh, right. Yes, I'm the only one around here who uses them. My brother owned a hot dog place in Albuquerque that went out of business. He gave me thousands of these things, I don't think I'll ever run out."

"Is it mostly locals who come by here or

tourists?"

"Locals, no. Everyone local comes to my house to get peppers when they want them, they get them in bulk. Here, we get either tourists or people who pass through from Coatimundi or Eagle Ridge for work or business."

Hugh nodded. "I know it was a long time ago, but is there someone, maybe a regular, who drives a white pickup truck? They would have come by a year ago, around the time of Rainy's death. Might have been wearing a hoodie."

The pepper man shook his head. "A white pickup truck around here? You might as well ask if I've seen a cactus lately. Same with the hoodie."

"I know it's a long shot," said Hugh. "But if anything comes to mind, I'm staying in Coatimundi. Or you can tell Kai Wauneka."

"I will. I wish I did know something, I'd love to see the man caught. All the women around here are scared. My wife and my mother are afraid to walk to the store. I'll put the word out that people can trust you."

Pep loaded up a bag of hatch chilies. Then they grabbed some Navajo tacos and headed back to the truck.

"You're not saying much," said Hugh.

"I know, I'm sorry. It's just—there's more than one killer running loose around here. Someone killed Rainy and the other women. And someone killed Jim and Denzer. I don't think either one of them is Red Clayton."

"Don't be sorry. You have good instincts, Violet Vaughn. You obviously have a gut feeling about this. What do you want to do?"

Violet pulled in a deep breath, then let it out slowly. "I'm having my dinner party this evening. But tomorrow I have a few more questions to ask, just to get this out of my system. If I don't find any answers, I'll let it go."

"I promised I'd be your wing man 'til the end," Hugh said.

"It doesn't feel like the end to me. Not yet."

Hugh's blue eyes twinkled as he gave her a playful nudge. "Well keep me posted."

CHAPTER 21

The twin deep dish pizzas, sizzling and hot, were a boon to everyone's spirits. Violet's creations were met with applause all around from her group of new friends. She concocted what she called Southwestern Deep Dish Pizza—a gooey blend of cheese, Hatch chilies, sausage and a sauce made from local tomatoes. Maven, Maddie, Kai, Grace, Hugh and Violet demolished the two savory pies.

Violet borrowed a long table from Maven, which she covered with a tablecloth and decorated with little jars of late-season wild flowers. The group spent a peaceful afternoon watching the last of the Mundi Madness crowd load up and pull out of the park. The now-absent gathering of RVs and trailers left an unobscured view of the desert vista, the saguaro cacti shooting their sage-green arms toward the pink and purple sky.

"Violet, this pizza is the best damn thing I've tasted in a long time," Maven declared. "In fact, it's given me an idea. Everyone—follow me!"

She got up from the table and, seeing everyone hesitate, said, "Come on—let's go!"

The group pushed their chairs back and followed Maven as she walked the gravel path back toward the motel, past the office and out to the street. Violet wondered what trick Maven had up her sleeve this time. Maven led the group across the road and they found themselves standing in front of a boarded-up old building. It appeared to be some kind of former business.

Maven rustled in her pocket and pulled out an enormous key ring.

Violet peered between the boards covering the windows. "What's this all about?"

"You'll see, you'll see," she said, fumbling through the keys. "Just go with me on this. Aha, here it is." She turned the lock. The front door, piled a foot high with tumbleweeds, trash and other debris, made a scratchy sound as it opened.

Gaps in the boards let in enough late-afternoon light to allow a dim view of the room. It looked like a restaurant from a ghost town. Tables and chairs sat frozen in time, some still holding salt, pepper and napkin holders, all frosted with cobwebs and dust. A menu board hung lopsided over an order counter, behind which hung three pizza pans labeled Small, Medium and Large. Debris had blown in under the door, leaving a thick coat of dirt and leaf meal on the floor.

"This—" Maven said, stretching her arms out, "used to be the only pizza place in Coatimundi. I own the property, but it's been closed for years. Benji Brown never could manage to run the place."

Maddie brought an imaginary bottle to her mouth and tilted it back. "More like drank away all the profits."

Maven chuckled. "True that. Poor Joan, she put up with his nonsense for far too long. The place could have been profitable, but half the time he was passed out in the back."

"Who's Joan?" Hugh asked.

"Joan Brown. You know, Jennifer Norris' mom."

The niggling feeling came back into Violet's brain, poking into the far reaches of her sensibilities. "I thought her name was Mrs. Norris?"

Maddie shook her head. "Used to be. That's her maiden name. She was, uh—an unwed mother when she married Benji."

Violet moved around the vacant old pizza place in a daze, looking at the black and white pictures on the wall and thinking. In the distance, she heard Maven chattering about the place.

"So, I was thinking—you make a damn fine pizza, Violet, and this place is just sitting empty. Of course, it needs some cleaning up, but we'll all help with that, and I could give you free rent 'til you're up and running."

Violet vaguely heard talk from the group and sounds of agreement from everyone. But there was a fuzzy, whomp whomp sound in her ears as adrenaline messed with her head. Her eyes had landed on a photo, a desert scene. In the distance, an old windmill stood guard over some cows and a crisscrossing of barbed wire fences. The structure was very similar to Jim's windmill. Something pinged in her gut. She spun around.

"Thanks Maven, this is all—really nice of you, I'll—I'll think about it. But, I have something I have to do right now, something I just remembered."

She turned to Hugh. "Can you take me out to Jim's place?"

"Right now? It's gonna be dark soon."

She was already moving toward the door, Spirit at her heels. She looked back to see the small group eyeing her, mouths open. "I really need my wingman on this one."

Hugh didn't hesitate. "Onward and upward!"

"You have no idea how right you are," she said, leading him out the door.

CHAPTER 22

"So what are we looking for?"

The last time Violet and Hugh trudged the path up to Jim's place it was daytime. Violet remembered the windmill squeaking and screaming in the breeze. This time, a quiet hung about the place, the evening air dead still. With the encroaching darkness, Violet thought she preferred the screeching.

"I don't want to say too much in case I'm wrong," said Violet. "Some of my hunches lately have been a little—out there. This is another one of those."

Spirit trotted along with them, his ears twitching and eyes sharp. He seemed to sense this was not playtime and he assumed a working dog's demeanor, alert to signs of danger.

The silver trailer up ahead reflected the clear, dusky sky. Behind it, the windmill loomed black and menacing. It seemed taller and more forbidding than Violet had remembered. Of course, it probably seemed taller—now that she knew what she had to do.

"We're looking for a ladder."

Hugh looked momentarily confused, and then

realization hit him. "Yes," he said. "Of course! Let's check around the base. And watch out for rattlesnakes."

"Do rattlesnakes come out at night?"

"I have no idea, we don't have rattlesnakes in the U.K. Let's err on the side of caution. Maven said not to overturn anything on the ground, that's where they like to hide."

"Noted," said Violet.

The windmill was built into a small hill behind the trailer, the ground below it covered with rocks and brush. They searched around for a ladder, but found nothing. Hugh decided to search near the trailer. Eventually, Violet heard a shout.

"Over here!"

Slightly underneath the back side of the trailer, flat to the ground, lay an old wooden ladder. Weeds and plants grew up through the rungs. It had obviously not been disturbed by the FBI forensic team, despite them tearing up a good portion of the property.

Hugh went to drag the ladder out. "Be careful," Violet whispered. She wasn't sure why she felt the need to whisper since they were the only ones out there.

He pulled the ladder out enough so that each of them could grab one end. Violet's arms strained under its weight. The old wood felt moist and cool in her hands from sitting next to the earth. Then she thought about scorpions. Maven had said there were scorpions out here too. She desperately hoped a scorpion was not near where her hand gripped the ladder.

They maneuvered it toward the windmill, finally turning it sideways, planting one end in the ground and leaning it up against the structure. It came to rest at the base of the wooden platform near the top. Violet cranked her head to look all the way up. She turned her phone flashlight on and stepped on the first rung.

"Let me go first," said Hugh, also turning on his flashlight.

"No, you stay and hold the base, make sure it's stable." She began to climb. The rungs felt solid, with just a slight creak with each step. She reached the platform and pulled herself up. A racket of flapping and squawking hit her as doves, startled from their nesting spot, flew in every direction. She ducked and let out a little screech.

"You okay?" Hugh called.

"Yes, just some birds that aren't too happy to see me."

"I'm coming up," he called.

She could see sporadic lights across the mesa and the twinkling of Coatimundi in the distance. Then she turned to examine the structure to see if her hunch was correct.

The four legs of the windmill came together to form a pyramid. From the platform, three feet up to the tip was covered in planks of wood, creating a hollow space inside.

You just have to remember what I told you, was

what Jim's letter said. No matter how much she racked her brain, the only thing she could remember him telling her about the property was that it had an old windmill. She had not realized the significance until she looked at the photo in the abandoned pizza parlor.

She shined her flashlight on the wooden planks. Hugh hoisted himself up and came to stand next to her. A bright, full moon had risen to light up the mesa.

"See anything?"

"All the boards look to be nailed down pretty tight. This one here is slightly loose. I should have thought to bring something to pry the boards off."

"You mean like this?" said Hugh, brandishing a Swiss Army knife.

"Of course, you would have a pocket knife, that is so—you."

"N.R.S., Gopher Level," he said with a wink.

"I'm sorry—what?"

"Nottingham Rover Scouts. I'll sing you The Preparedness Song some other time, when we're not 50 feet up in the air."

He slipped the knife under the edge of the loose board and began to wiggle it. He was able to pull it out enough that they could get their fingers under the edge and pull. Finally, the wooden plank came free, the two long nails still attached, looking like rattlesnake fangs.

Hugh held his flashlight to the gap and Violet peered inside.

"It looks like—there's a big lump. It's a tarp. We'll need to take out more planks."

The two worked for several minutes, loosening boards with the knife and pulling them off one by one until there was enough room to reach inside. Hugh sat down and maneuvered himself slightly inside. He used his knife to slash the blue tarp.

The covering fell away and they both gasped. Money. Stacks and stacks of bundles of money. Hugh grabbed a packet and they examined it up close.

"They're hundreds," Violet whispered. "This—is a lot of money."

She could hear Spirit barking down below. He must be wondering what the heck we are doing, she thought.

"I need to get a hold of Montoya right away," Violet said.

"You don't have any thought of keeping it for yourself? Buying a villa in Europe?"

Her heart pounded with the exhilaration of the find, and the triumph of being right. She briefly flitted through scenarios in her mind—sitting on a tropical beach with a fruity cocktail, gambling in Monaco, shopping in Beverly Hills.

"No. Most of it belongs to Jim's victims. I'll feel a lot better when things are finally set right." She put out a hand to help Hugh up from his crouched position and he held onto it for a moment.

"That's the right thing to do."

"Yes. Now I can put the ghost of Jim to rest."

Spirit's barking had now reached a high and continuous pitch. Violet stepped to the edge of the platform to call down to him. But what she saw made her freeze in place. All that came out of her mouth was a startled little gasp as her blood ran cold. There was nowhere to run.

"Put your hands up, Mrs. Vaughn. You too, Englishman. Step where I can see you."

Joan Brown stood in the silvery moonlight, feet planted hip width apart. There was no mistaking the shotgun trained directly at Violet and Hugh. Violet was certain she knew how to use it.

CHAPTER 23

"This is what's gonna happen," Joan shouted up to them. "Start throwing the money down, Mrs. Vaughn. If you try anything funny, I'm gonna send the Englishman to visit the Queen. And drop your phones down too. Let's go."

Violet felt frozen to the spot, her mind racing to find a way out of the situation. Spirit's barks had turned to growls and snarls as he faced off with the intruder.

"Call your dog off, or he's gonna get it," Joan yelled.

The threat to Spirit spurred Violet into action. She knew what Joan was capable of. With a quavering voice, she called down to her dog. "Spirit, it's okay, buddy, it's okay."

Spirit looked up at Violet uncertainly and back at Joan. He maintained his aggressive stance but quit barking for the time being.

"We'd better do as she says, for now," Hugh whispered. "We're defenseless up here."

"Drop your phones down!"

Violet reluctantly dropped her phone over the edge and heard it hit with a thump. Hugh fumble with his and dropped it over the side. Violet went to the opening and felt around in the darkness for the money pile. She began pulling out stacks of bills and setting them on the platform. Hugh picked them up and tossed them down. It seemed like forever getting through the stack. As she worked, Violet tried to think of a plan to get away. It wasn't likely Joan was going to let them go, not after this.

"Okay, that's the last of it," Violet called down when she reached the bottom of the money pile. "Now take the money and go." She came to stand next to Hugh on the edge of the platform. They clutched hands.

"Try to stall," Hugh whispered under his breath. Then he leaned over the platform.

"Mrs. Brown. If you pull the ladder down, we'll be stuck up here until tomorrow, maybe longer. You'll have plenty of time to get away."

"Nice try," she said flatly. "Now climb down the ladder. Let's go."

Without any choice, Violet climbed down and Hugh followed. Each step felt like a moment closer to their doom. Joan had killed before, she had nothing to lose. Despite the chill evening air, Violet's hands and brow were sweating. At the bottom, they turned to face Joan and the shotgun, which, up close, appeared even larger. Despite her diminutive stature, Joan appeared to have a solid hold on it. Bundles of money littered the ground, the pale stacks glowing in the moonlight.

Spirit came to stand in front of Violet, low growls rumbling in his throat. Hugh said they needed to stall, he must have some kind of plan. She hoped so, because she had nothing—they were out in the desert at night, miles away from anyone. Even gunshots would go unnoticed out here. She remembered when they were in the Sunset Title office, how easy it was to get Joan talking about her past.

"J.N. Brown," Violet said, trying to muster some confidence into her voice. "Joan Norris Brown. You're the one that notarized my home sale documents. You knew Jim forged my name. But I'm not sure why you would agree to put yourself at risk that way, for him."

"I thought you might figure that out eventually," said Joan, shaking her head. "That's why I searched your place—I was looking for the escrow papers. You hadn't said anything, so I figured you must not have put two and two together, yet."

"And you stole my boots."

"Yes. When I didn't find what I was looking for, I thought the papers might still be at Jim's place. I figured I might as well wear your boots and frame you for the break-in. Catch two coati with one trap, as my dad used to say."

Violet shuddered. Trapped is exactly what they were. Trapped by a mad woman with no foreseeable way out. She nudged closer to Hugh and hoped they could avoid being the two ill-fated coati in the story. She still had to keep Joan going. "But that still doesn't explain why you would do it—what was in it for you?"

"I think I have the answer to that," said Hugh. "When Jim first walked into Sunset Title, you saw an opportunity. Your daughter Jennifer was back in town after her divorce. In your mind, Jennifer had never gotten what was due to her, right? Because she's a Clayton, isn't she? You had to watch her take second place to all the Claytons when she was actually one of them."

Joan looked momentarily startled, and lowered the gun from her shoulder to her waist, eyes narrowed. "Dwight Clayton." She spat out the words. "He's the one who sold Jim this property. He was a piece of work."

She lifted her chin and raised her eyes to the sky. "Oh, but he did sweep me off my feet. He told me he was gonna leave his wife and make me queen of the Clayton ranch. We would meet in the sheep barns. He'd play music and we'd dance and dance." Joan began to sway side to side and then whirl around with the gun, as if she were back in the barn, dancing with Dwight.

Hugh and Violet side-eyed each other and Violet knew he was thinking the same as she—craaazy.

Violet was just about to jump up and try to grab the gun, but Joan snapped out of her reverie and swung the shotgun back toward them, making Violet flinch and Spirit bark. "I was young and stupid and I fell for his crap. Of course, when I got pregnant, it was a different story."

"He wouldn't leave his wife and left you an unwed mother in a very small town," said Hugh.

"It doesn't take a genius to figure that out, doctor." Joan said. "But you're right—and I should have known better. That wasn't the only thing. He threatened me. Told me if I breathed a word to anyone, he'd ruin my family's business. So I had to watch those Claytons prancing around town like they owned it—while Jennifer and I got nothing."

As Joan was talking, Violet had managed to get a toe on her cell phone and was gradually inching it closer. When it was almost directly below her, Joan leapt forward and kicked the phone. It went sailing into the darkness.

"Plain little Joan's not so slow, is she? No one even knows I exist. I'm invisible. But that doesn't mean I'm stupid. I've had plenty of time to plan my revenge on the Claytons. It hasn't worked out exactly as I'd hoped, but I'm thinking it might be even better. Red Clayton's going to prison and I've got the money —thanks to the both of you." She began to do another little dance. She really is off her rocker, Violet thought. That doesn't bode well for us.

"You two," Joan snapped, once again displaying a split-second personality change. "Sit down on the ground, back to back." She saw them hesitate and brandished the gun. "Do it!"

They sat back to back as Joan commanded. Violet could feel the warmth and strength of Hugh's back. The thought floated through her mind that if she was going to die, she was glad to have met Hugh. The brief time knowing him had made her feel like a new person, at least for a little while. Her old self, sad and withdrawn, plodded through each day, thinking that was all she deserved or was capable of—afraid of getting close to others and afraid of getting hurt.

Hugh made her feel smart and funny and valued. Oh how she wished she could feel that way a little longer.

"Mrs. Brown," Hugh said. "Your feelings of being invisible are normal, especially as we get older."

Joan let out a cackling laugh. "It's a little late for the psychology, doctor. I've already forged documents, committed burglary, framed a man, and—as you've probably figured out— killed two people."

"It doesn't make sense why you killed Jim and Denzer," said Violet, trying again to stall for time. Joan appeared to be easily distracted. If they kept her going, maybe they could figure out a way to jump her and grab the gun.

"I didn't set out to kill anyone—I'm not a psychopath," hissed Joan, standing over them with the gun. Violet begged to differ on that one.

"When I first met Jim and he was flashing his money around, I thought he'd be a good match for Jennifer. Then I found out he owned the piece of land the Claytons were all worked up over. They'd been to my office over the years, wanting to know who owned it and if they could buy it back. A genuine piece of the Clayton ranch, owned by an outsider—that really riled them up. With Jim's money and the land, Jennifer could build up her own place—that would really stick it to the Claytons. I spent so many hours thinking about that, picturing Red Clayton coming to beg us to sell him the land and sending him away empty handed."

If Joan pictured herself becoming a great land baroness—by proxy anyway, she certainly had picked the wrong man to pin her hopes on, Violet thought.

"Jim started taking Jennifer out, spending a bunch of money on her," Joan continued. I thought my plans were falling into place. I didn't realize I was the sucker—that I was no match for him."

"I could write a book," said Violet.

"Shut up!" yelled Joan, pointing the shotgun at her. "If it wasn't for you—"

Spirit leapt at Joan, growling and snarling and nearly knocked her over. Joan kicked at him and Violet was terrified she would shoot him. She called him and he came to sit at her feet, eyes trained on Joan.

"Jim tricked you, didn't he?" Violet said, trying to get Joan's attention off Spirit.
"He sensed your interest and told you he couldn't move here until he sold his house in Chicago—but his ex wife's name was on the title. I'm sure he didn't mention he was still married, because you might not have helped him. He convinced you to notarize my fake signature on the sale document, which you did, hoping to get in tight with him. But once you did, he had something over your head."

Joan scowled. "You know how he operates. He moved that fancy trailer out to his property and that was the end of throwing money around. Jennifer spent time with him out there, still hoping he would marry her and she'd be a rich woman. She told me one time she found some storage bins full of cash. She said there must have been millions of dollars out here.

That's when I first came up with the idea. You know, of killing him. I figured after he and Jennifer got married, he could run into some kind of accident, step on a snake or something."

"Was Jennifer in on it?" Hugh asked.

"No!" she snapped. "I already told you, my Jennifer couldn't hurt a fly. She'd had enough of Jim after awhile and wanted to leave. But I kept encouraging her to stay, to work it out. You think that makes me a bad mother, don't you?" She glared fiercely from Violet to Hugh who both said nothing.

"I told her to tell him if he wasn't gonna marry her, she was leaving. And he *laughed* at her. Told her he never had any intention of marrying her, he was still married and would never divorce his wife." She pointed the gun at Violet. "You."

"So you went to confront him," said Hugh.

"I went there, but he laughed at me too. Told me he already had what he needed from me and if I didn't leave him alone, he'd report me for fraud. I didn't know at the time he was on the lam himself. I was gonna stop there. I was. But when I left, I looked down the road toward the Clayton place and I remembered. All those nights in the sheep barn with Dwight. There's all sorts of weapons laying around, they use them on the ranch, for coyotes and snakes. So I snuck on the property and found what I was looking for."

"That's how you got Red Clayton's gun and knife," said Hugh.

"I took *two* guns and a knife. I used the knife to go back and kill Jim, of course. Stabbed him right in his sleep, easy as pie. I planned to take all the cash, find Jennifer and leave town. I tore that place apart. But I couldn't find the money. I saw headlights down the drive so I ran out of there. I figured I'd have time to go back the next morning and search—but then *you* showed up."

"The P.I., Denzer. He must have seen you," said Violet.

"He saw me leaving that night and got a good look at me and my car. I followed him back to the motel, and—well, you know—did him in."

Joan's total lack of remorse in killing the innocent P.I. sent a shiver down Violet's spine and she heard Hugh gasp. She likely would have no remorse at killing them either.

"The other gun is this one," Joan said, waving the shotgun in the air. When they find the two of you, they'll think one of the Claytons came out here and attacked you. I might even bring down the whole Clayton family by the time I'm done."

She broke into maniacal laughter and started another one of her dances. Spirit took that opportunity to lunge at Joan, growling. He managed to catch her off guard and sunk his teeth into her leg, causing Joan to squeal and curse. An explosion sounded as the gun went off. Spirit yelped and stumbled into the darkness.

"No!" Violet cried. "No! Spirit!"

Violet fell backwards as all of sudden, Hugh

wasn't there anymore. He leapt toward Joan and they fought over the gun. The shot rendered Violet partially deaf. Everything sounded fuzzy and seemed to be moving in slow motion. All she could think about was Spirit. She had questioned her abilities to be a good caretaker to the dog, but when the gun went off and she heard his yelp of pain, she felt like her entire world had crashed down. But now Hugh was in trouble too and needed her help.

Violet pushed herself up and stumbled to where Hugh was still struggling with Joan. The squirrely woman was not going down without a fight. Both had hands on the gun. Hugh tripped over some of the money and lost his grasp, stumbling and nearly falling down. Joan whirled and aimed the gun at him. Violet grabbed a rock off the ground and palmed it, ready to strike the cardigan-wearing crazy woman from behind. But Joan heard her and swung the gun around. Violet felt a crack on her head and things became fuzzier and fuzzier as she slumped to the ground.

She found herself fighting to stay conscious. She felt heavy as blackness began to close around her. No, she thought, I can't leave Hugh...and Spirit. No, it's not the end. Then there were voices coming closer and closer and a bright light bouncing through the darkness. The last thing she heard before she lost consciousness was a single word.

"Freeze!"

CHAPTER 24

"Violet...I don't think she can hear me." Hugh's voice floated in from far away, warm and comforting, like her favorite quilt, no—like a deep dish pizza. She felt hungry. Where was she? Didn't she just make some pizza? Someone held her hands and rubbed them vigorously. She opened her eyes and found herself staring up at Hugh's concerned face and someone else—Montoya.

"Spirit," Violet said, but it came out as a dry whisper.

Montoya patted her arm. "He's gonna be okay, Mrs. Vaughn. Dr. Wauneka is treating him right now. It looks like he was just grazed. He'll be alright."

Blue and red lights flashed off the shiny airstream trailer. Sheriff Winters, hands on hips, talked to someone sitting on the ground. Joan Brown. Then everything came back to her.

"I want to see Spirit," she said, "He saved us, he's a good dog, he's—"

"The paramedics just showed up," said Hugh. "You took a blow to the head—you need to go to hospital. I'll take care of Spirit."

Montoya motioned the paramedics over, then hurried off, talking into her phone. Violet squeezed Hugh's hand. "How did they know we were out here?"

"When Joan first told us to throw our phones down, I hit redial on the last number I called, which happened to be Kai Wauneka. He heard everything and kept the line open while he got help."

"We made it," Violet whispered, squeezing Hugh's hand even tighter.

"Yes," said Hugh. "We did. Now you have to stay. It's—destiny."

"We'll see," she whispered. "We'll see."

The Coatimundi hospital, a small, white building out behind the sheriff's office, was overseen by Dr. Tamara Goodwill, a no-nonsense woman who travelled between several rural clinics. Violet found herself in a square room with two beds on each side and a scattering of chairs and side tables. Picture windows offered glorious views of the desert. Instead of plain, clinical blankets, each bed was adorned with a hand-made quilt, which, Maven told her, were made by the Coatimundi Sewing Club.

After one night in the hospital she felt ready to return to her RV and see Spirit. But Dr. Goodwill said she needed observation for another day. Now, she was surrounded with visitors, flowers and, thankfully, food. Grace brought her a Navajo taco, Maven and Maddie brought a plate of ribs, and Hugh brought some of her own leftover deep dish pizza.

She reached up and felt her bare scalp where her

head had been shaved to allow for stitches. Her nose crinkled as she felt the fairly large patch.

"I have all sorts of hats you can borrow," said Maven from an armchair under the window.

"No," said Maddie, as she lounged on one of the empty beds. "If she's gonna be a real Southwestern woman, she needs her own cowboy hat."

Hugh sat in a chair right next to the bed. "I think a Sherlock Holmes hat is more her style. She's the one who cracked the case."

"How did you suspect Joan Brown?" asked Kai, who leaned against the wall, a rib in his hand.

Violet and Hugh filled them in on the details of their adventure and close call.

"There's just one thing I still haven't solved," said Violet, looking at Hugh. "The RED written in C.J. Denzer's notebook."

"I think I figured that out," said Hugh. "Joan left her car on the road near Jim's place. There's a big logo on the side. Sunset Title, R.E.D.—Real Estate Documents. When he caught a glimpse of her car, that's all he had time to scribble down."

There was a tap on the door, and Montoya came in, along with Sheriff Winters and Deputy Jones.

"Uh-oh, here comes the fuzz," said Maven.

"We need a few moments with Mrs. Vaughn," said Montoya.

Everyone cleared out with waves and promises to see Violet soon. Hugh planted a kiss on her forehead. "Get well, Violet Vaughn."

All three law enforcement officers looked tired

and dusty. Violet imagined while she was getting a good night's sleep, the three of them had probably been out working the crime scene and processing Joan.

"Sheriff Winters is here to get a statement," said Montoya. "But I wanted to come and thank you —for finding the money. It's really going to help Jim's victims. And for me, personally—you helped me close out my case. I've talked to some people in the home office, and they said you can take possession of the property—but you probably won't see any of the money. At least not for a long time."

Violet nodded. She hadn't even expected the property.

"Mrs. Vaughn," said Sheriff Winters, tilting his head at her.

"What happened to Deep Dish?" asked Violet. "I was getting used to the name."

"I was—wrong," said the Sheriff. There followed a long silence in which Violet determined that was all the apology she was going to get from him.

"Montoya—I mean, *Special Agent* Montoya and I have more work to do, so Jones will take a statement. Take care, Mrs. Vaughn. It's been—interesting."

A smile tweaked the corners of her mouth as she watched him go. I'll be seeing you sooner than you think, she thought. He hasn't seen the last of Deep Dish.

CHAPTER 25

Violet pushed a large piece of kitchen equipment aside and then let out an earsplitting scream. She jumped up on the stainless steel island in the middle of the kitchen with lightning speed, just as the double doors flew open and a crowd of people flooded in, led by Hugh.

"What happened, are you alright?" he said, taking her hand.

"Sc—sc—scorpion!" Violet pointed to the corner. Maven went over to investigate.

"This scorpion is deader than Coatimundi on a Wednesday in November."

"Oh," said Violet. "Sorry."

Good natured laughs rang out as some people went to check out the dead bug and others went back to their work.

Violet felt grateful and amazed how many people turned out to help with the cleanup of the new restaurant. Hugh, of course, and Maven and Maddie. Kai and Grace drove in from White Feather bringing a bunch of friends, including Dr. Pepper and his wife.

Violet's jaw dropped with surprise when Montoya showed up. Within a short time, the FBI agent took charge of the group, assigning tasks and "stations" as she called them. Violet noticed Montoya assigned herself to work together with Kai, and they were seen joking around—and dare Violet say—flirting.

Both Violet and her dog had bald patches that were now beginning to re-grow hair, their wounds healing over. But her head was covered with a beautiful new cowboy hat, a gift from Kai and Grace. Made from tan-colored straw, a leather band encircled the crown with three tawny feathers adorning the side.

"Great Horned Owl feathers," Kai told her.

Violet sucked in her breath, remembering the late night visitor.

"I heard him in the trees, when we were at your place. They symbolize wisdom, so I thought it was fitting."

"I will treasure it," she told him. "But I'm not sure if wisdom fits me."

Kai placed the hat on her head. "Wisdom isn't inherent. It's hard fought."

Earlier in the day, Red Clayton stopped by the restaurant, the back of his pickup truck filled with cases of beer, wine and soda.

"I owe you one," he said to Violet and Hugh. "I owe you more than one, actually, I owe you my life. I brought a few things to get you started here. Now, Mrs. Vaughn—Violet, can I call you Violet? Have you thought any more about selling the land to me? You can build a big old fancy house with what I can pay you—" and off he went with his sales pitch.

Truth was, she had started picturing herself living on the mesa—on what was now her own land. For better or worse, Coatimundi had gotten under her skin. Liberated from Jim, she was taking giant steps toward realizing who she was and who she could be —and how important a support system is in that process.

Absent from the group were Sheriff Winters and Jennifer Norris. Violet could imagine Jennifer was going through a tough time. Naturally, her mother was the talk of the entire county and beyond. Some folks even speculated that Jennifer had known what her mother was up to, or had even been involved. Violet thought Jennifer was just as much a victim of Joan and Jim as any of the others.

There might have been a silver lining for Jennifer. Violet had seen her and the sheriff walking hand in hand down Main Street, quite obviously in complete love. Jennifer, liberated from her overbearing mother, could finally do as she wished. She had taken over Sunset Title and was planning on renovating and modernizing it. It remained to be seen if she would form a relationship with her newfound Clayton kin.

As for Sheriff Winters, Violet hadn't spoken to him since she was in the hospital. But she was certain he knew about the restaurant and that she was in Coatimundi to stay. Next week her new sign would arrive. The genuine neon work of art, hand-crafted by a friend of Maven's, would be a simple design featuring the restaurant's name—Deep Dish. How she wished she could see the sheriff's face the first time he drove by.

Now, she sat out back of the restaurant, taking a break with Hugh and watching Spirit run and play. They lounged in folding chairs, legs outstretched, drinking some wine and enjoying the view. The mesa stretched out before them in all its complex wonder —barren, yet full of life, beautiful, yet dangerous. She looked over at Hugh and felt a sensation she was trying to get used to—a feeling of things being right with the world. "You know that painting at Red Clayton's place, the one of Kokopelli?"

Hugh nodded. "The god of agriculture?"

"Actually, he's also the god of birth. In my case, re-birth. Coming to this place, right from the start, I felt re-born. You don't really know what it is to belong until you actually do. You know what I mean?"

Hugh reached over and took her hand and held it in both of his, like he was cradling a baby bird. "Yes, he said. I think I do."

THE END

Made in the USA
Las Vegas, NV
15 April 2024

88730701R00105